This book is for Carys Eloise — T.B.
With love to Mason — K.L.

The artwork in this book was created primarily using chalk pastel, ink and watercolour on paper with the occasional use of acrylic paint.

First published in 2024 by Floris Books. First published in the USA in 2025
Second printing 2024. Text © 2024 Theresa Breslin. Illustrations © 2024 Kate Leiper
Theresa Breslin and Kate Leiper have asserted their right under the Copyright, Designs
and Patent Act 1988 to be identified as the Author and Illustrator of this Work
All rights reserved. No part of this book may be reproduced without the prior permission
of Floris Books, Edinburgh www.florisbooks.co.uk British Library CIP data available
ISBN 978-178250-910-3 Printed in China through Asia Pacific Offset Ltd

An Illustrated
Treasury of
Dragon
Tales

Stories from
Around the World

Theresa Breslin **Kate Leiper**

Floris
Books

Contents

Héhuā and Her Golden Dragon-Boy
China — 9

The Dragon of Kinnoull Meets St Serf
Scotland — 21

The Dragon Apep Fights the Sun God Ra
Egypt — 39

Smok, the Seven-Headed Dragon of Krakow
Poland — 55

Kukulkan, the Dragon God of Yucatán
Mexico — 69

Jörmungandr, the Dragon Son of Loki
Scandinavia — 83

The Three Dragons of Peterhof Palace
Russia — 95

The Dragon of Colchis, Guardian of the Golden Fleece
Greece — 115

Toyotama-hime, Dragon Princess of the Sea
Japan — 135

Lord Krishna and Kaliya Naag
India — 149

Héhuā and Her Golden Dragon-Boy

In ancient Chinese culture the dragon is a legendary creature with divine powers. It is connected to the number nine, which, in Chinese, sounds like 'everlasting'. Worshipped as a god, the dragon brings good luck and wealth and can grant special favours, but only to those who are worthy of receiving them.

This story is a retelling of a very old folk tale linked to the famous Chinese Dragon Dance.

Héhuā: *huh-**hwah***   Cūn Zhǎng: *sun-jong*

Long, long ago in a remote village in China there lived a girl called Héhuā.

Like the lotus flower after which she was named, Héhuā was bright to behold. Just as lotus flowers bloom in a variety of colours, so Héhuā liked to wear clothes in rose pink, pale yellow, lilac and white.

Héhuā had a thoughtful mind and a kind soul. Thus, when she grew up, more than one suitor wanted to marry her. Héhuā chose an older man who was poor but honourable.

They lived together in peace and joy, and, as the months went on, Héhuā hoped to have a baby.

"I wish I had a darling little child to care for and cuddle," she said to herself. "By day, I would carry my baby beside the river and point out the fish and the birds. At night, I would sing them to sleep under the silver moon." When she'd been married for nine hundred and ninety-nine days, Héhuā decided to ask the Dragon God to grant her wish.

From a piece of willow wood, she carved a tiny dragon statue to make a shrine for the Dragon God in her house. Every nine days Héhuā laid lotus blossoms there.

And it seemed to her that the tiny wooden dragon smiled in return.

Nine hundred and ninety-nine days later, Héhuā found that she was indeed going to have a baby. On the day that celebrates the Dragon God, Héhuā gave birth to a healthy boy.

Sadly, not long after this, Héhuā's husband passed away. At the shrine she prayed for her husband and asked the Dragon God to help guard her child and keep him from harm.

And it seemed to her that the tiny wooden dragon smiled in return.

For nine hundred and ninety-nine days Héhuā tended her child as he learned to sit up and toddle about.

In the daytime, Héhuā carried the baby beside the river and pointed to the fish and the birds. At night she sang him to sleep under the silver moon. In the evenings, when she took him to bathe in the river, Héhuā noticed the skin on his back glowing pale amber.

During the following nine hundred and ninety-nine days, Héhuā saw the skin turn tawny and begin to crackle softly. She tried not to dwell upon this, being content to cuddle her son close and place her trust in the Dragon God to shield him.

Over the next nine hundred and ninety-nine days, the child's tawny skin separated into what appeared to be tiny overlapping glittering leaves.

On his ninth birthday, Héhuā examined them carefully. Then she knelt down and gazed in wonderment.

Her son's back was covered in nine hundred and ninety-nine golden dragon scales!

Héhuā's first thought was how blessed she was. She had been gifted a son clearly favoured by the Dragon God. But Héhuā was sensible enough to know that this could make her child vulnerable. In particular, she thought of the village chief, the Cūn Zhǎng, who was cruel and greedy for money. He made the people pay heavy taxes, claiming they were for road mending and sewage disposal, but instead he bought sweetmeats and fancy clothes for himself.

So now, each evening, Héhuā waited until the riverbank was deserted before she went there. She and her son sheltered under a willow tree whose branches reached to the ground and overhung the water. Héhuā's neighbours believed her to be over-protective because she only had one child, and they merely smiled at her behaviour. However, the Cūn Zhǎng suspected that Héhuā was hiding something precious, and he began to keep watch on her.

And so it was that, after spying on the two of them for nine evenings, he caught sight of gold shining in the dusk.

"Aha!" the chief cried, tearing apart the curtain foliage of the willow tree. "Héhuā, I've found out your secret! You pretend to be poor, but you have a child of golden treasure!"

"No! No!" Héhuā cowered in fright. "I have done nothing wrong. This child was sent to me by the Dragon God."

"The Dragon God would not favour someone as humble as you in this way!" the Cūn Zhǎng scoffed. "Everyone knows how much you wanted a child. You must have stolen a baby! This golden boy is not yours." He stretched to take the child.

Héhuā screamed and, grabbing her son's hand, ran home to stand with him in front of the shrine of the Dragon God. "You know the truth of this matter," she whispered. "My son is my own. I did not steal him. Please help me!"

And it seemed to her that the tiny wooden dragon smiled in return.

At that moment, the door of the house crashed open and the Cūn Zhǎng towered in the threshold. He expected the woman and child to cringe before him. But Héhuā had drawn strength from her prayers, and she recalled that the lotus flower is a symbol of honour, and known for its fortitude. Héhuā resolved to be strong like the flower after which she was named, and she stepped in front of her child to protect him.

The Cūn Zhǎng pushed her roughly aside.

Suddenly a terrifying thunderclap rent the air, followed by a blinding burst of golden light as if the sun itself had crashed through the house roof.

The Cūn Zhǎng dropped to his knees, eyes wide in disbelief.

Héhuā's child had transformed into an awesome dragon-boy, with claws and spiky swishing tail. Scales of burnished gold clad his whole body. Opening his mouth, he spat forth bright-blue sparks.

The Cūn Zhǎng turned and ran.

Then the dragon-boy shot a flicker of red-hot flame after the fleeing man to set alight the seat of his trousers.

Yelping and yowling, the Cūn Zhǎng headed for the river and cool water. The villagers, alerted by the noise, gathered to chase him. They'd had enough of this Cūn Zhang, and they pursued him right across the river and out of the village.

The people were pleased to be rid of the cruel chief. Knowing Héhuā to be both sensible and kind, they elected her as their new Cūn Zhǎng. They were also pleased to have the dragon-boy in their midst, for he was as kind and wise as his mother. On dull days, to help their crops grow, he would turn his back so that his nine-hundred and ninety-nine golden scales reflected the rays of the sun, giving heat and light.

This story has been connected to the Dragon Dance performed in Chinese communities all over the world at Chinese New Year. Ancient tradition was that the long paper dragon held up by the dancers is chasing after a ball painted in the same lotus colours Héhuā loved to wear.

Chinese New Year, being a spring festival, is a renewal of hope, and a celebration of life and family – with the dragon as a symbol of strength and good fortune.

The Dragon of Kinnoull Meets St Serf

A manuscript written many centuries ago tells of a most horrible dragon. This most horrible dragon terrorised everybody living around Kinnoull, in Perthshire, Scotland. According to local legend, the people were saved by a holy man named Serf, who went to meet the dragon and bravely 'smote the loathsome beast'.
But perhaps Serf had a little help…

In the sixth century, the Great Wood of Caledon stretched across a vast area of Scotland. Over rugged mountains and through green glens, trees grew in abundance: mighty oak and hardy pine, cedar and beech, aspen and ancient yew, juniper and rowan.

The forest near the Hill of Kinnoull gave shelter to all manner of life – a home for bears and wolves and wildcats, for roe deer and red deer. It was also home to Broca, the woodcutter's daughter. Broca was a sturdy and talented lass. She chopped firewood, split kindling, and could whittle and carve the most amazing wooden creatures.

Broca had lived her whole life in the woods, and so when she opened their hut door one bright sunny morning, she was quick to sense a change in the air.

"Looks like it's going to be another lovely day," said her father.

"I don't think so," Broca replied, wrinkling her nose.

"What's up, lass?" Her father came to stand beside her.

Broca knew the smells of the forest: the tang of pine, the scent of fir, the aroma of applewood. What was wafting on the wind was none of these. She frowned, then said:

"Something is burning."

Forest fires are very dangerous. Thus the woods already had firebreaks and water channels, and piles of long-handled brooms to beat down smouldering sparks and embers.

Broca hurried with her father to the village meeting place, where people had collected brooms and buckets of water. They moved swiftly towards a plume of smoke that was rising into the sky. As they drew nearer, ahead of them, around the base of a tree, flames were burning with a strange luminous glow.

Broca's father spoke fearfully. "I've never seen it before myself, but that could be dragon-fire."

"What would cause it?" one of the villagers asked.

"A dragon," Broca replied. "Obviously."

"We don't get dragons in these parts."

"We do now," said Broca, and pointed to the top of a massive oak tree.

Looming above the branches was a huge dragon.

The ground shuddered as the beast came thundering straight at them. Yellow eyes glared from below hooded lids, and its snarling jaws were agape, revealing rows of jagged teeth. The dragon's black tongue snaked out, and with it a scarlet scorching burst of flames.

Broca yanked on her father's arm and dragged him into a nearby bush. Everyone else dropped their buckets and brooms and ran home in terror, shrieking and yelling. The dragon crashed after them, set fire to a few barns, snatched some haystacks to munch, then lolloped off in the direction of Kinnoull Hill.

Broca and her father watched as the dragon made for a deep cave in the rocks.

"It's going to make a den for itself," Broca's father said in a worried voice. "It intends to stay in Kinnoull."

"Forever?" Broca asked him.

"Once the beast settles in, it'll take a miracle to move it out."

That evening the villagers planned a hunting party to slay the dragon. But Broca had been close enough to the creature to see that its hide was well protected.

"Spears and arrows will bounce off its scales," she said.

"We have never failed yet to bring down a wild beast," the hunters replied.

"There's always a first time," said Broca. "I hope you can run fast."

Fortunately, the hunters *could* run fast, for their weapons bounced off the dragon and they were forced to retreat rapidly from Kinnoull Hill.

"This time we'll trap it with our nets," they said at the next meeting.

But Broca had seen the dragon's sharp claws, great jaws and strong teeth.

"Nets will be torn to pieces," she said.

"We have never failed yet to trap a wild beast," the hunters replied.

"There's always a first time," said Broca. "I hope you can run *really* fast."

Fortunately, the hunters *could* run really fast, for the dragon tore their trapping nets and rampaged about, gathering up hens and sheep and geese and grain before tottering back to its den.

During the third meeting the hunters resolved to build a high barricade to encircle the village and trust that the dragon would shortly move on somewhere else.

As they said this, Broca recalled the words of her father: *Once the beast settles in, it'll take a miracle to move it out.*

Now, Broca had heard tell of a holy man named Serf who lived a few miles away in Dunning and was noted for his praying and preaching. There had been talk that this man might even be a saint who could work miracles. But when Broca mentioned asking the holy man for assistance, nobody paid any attention.

Later, walking home with her father, Broca said, "Apart from improving the running skills of our hunters, we are no further forwards in solving the dragon problem. I, myself, will find the holy man, Serf, and bring him to Kinnoull."

"You are a fine capable lass, Broca," said her father, laying his hand on her shoulder. "You go, and I'll help build the barricade."

So, the following morning Broca set out on the road to Dunning.

In his kitchen garden, the holy man, Serf, listened to Broca and said that he'd be happy to help get rid of the dragon who was robbing and terrorising the village of Kinnoull.

"I'll say a special prayer each morning," Serf promised.

"I don't think that will be enough," said Broca.

"At noon too, then," said Serf. "That should do it. Don't you agree?"

"No," Broca replied. This conversation wasn't going the way she'd expected.

"How about morning, noon and night?" suggested Serf.

"I was hoping that you'd come to Kinnoull and deal with it in person."

"Is it a big dragon?" Serf asked.

"*Enormous*," said Broca, for she was a truthful lass.

"Oh dear," said Serf.

"I thought this was what you did. Fixing problems for folk, working miracles."

"My role is providing leadership – guiding people on the path of goodness by example."

28

"If you smite the dragon, that would provide leadership," said Broca.

"Smite!" Serf exclaimed. "Do we need to actually kill it? Usually I just help crops grow, settle arguments and cure minor ailments."

"You'd be famous," said Broca, "part of Scotland's history: how Serf bravely smote the loathsome beast."

Serf sighed. "I suppose I could come and use gentle persuasion. Within every living creature is some tenderness – a soft spot." He wandered over to his rows of vegetables, murmuring to them to behave while he was gone, and not bicker amongst themselves as to who had the best position in the sun.

It was Broca's turn to say, "Oh dear." Serf's manner did not bode well for dragon-slaying, but at least the holy man was coming to Kinnoull.

As they reached the Hill of Kinnoull, Broca was glad to see the barricade was secure and the village was untouched. However, all the land around it was a trail of ruin and destruction.

"What a mess!" Serf tutted. "The poor creature must be awfully distressed."

"Couldn't you simply wave your hands and make this dragon go away?" asked Broca.

"I can't perform a miracle by snapping my fingers," said Serf. He paused, snapped his fingers, then when nothing happened, he went on, "I'll visit its den, speak a few words to the dragon and pray over it."

Broca did not think this was in any way a smart plan. With a sinking heart she realised that the holy man had no idea of the danger involved in approaching the dragon without a weapon.

So, while Serf was preparing himself, she went to the forest and chopped wood from a hazel tree. She expertly whittled until she'd smoothed a staff, with a solid root knot at the top that fitted snugly into a clasped hand.

"Have this." She offered the staff to Serf. "In case the dragon refuses to do as you ask."

Serf shook his head. "I shall use my most caring sermon," he declared, "to coax the beast into desisting from its wickedness."

"Don't you think that a stout staff might have more effect than soft speech?"

"I'd rather not be armed when I meet the creature," Serf replied. "Brandishing a club might give the wrong impression – start us off on the wrong foot."

"It's a *dragon*." Broca indicated the village's crushed cattle sheds and frazzled crops.

"Nevertheless…" Serf smiled at her. "I can't go ahead and bash your dragon's skull without giving it a chance to mend its ways. It's not, not… very *nice*, is it?"

Broca thought quickly. "Think of it more as a walking stick." She crossed her fingers behind her back to counter the fact that she was fibbing to a holy person. "You can lean on it as you climb the hill." Thrusting the wooden staff into Serf's hand, she added quickly, "It's impolite to reject a gift."

"That's true." Reluctantly, Serf accepted the staff. "But I will not wield brute force upon the beast."

Serf took the hillside track. Broca decided she'd better follow him.

Wanting to witness the spectacle, but keeping a safe distance, the village folk straggled after them.

When Serf drew near to the dragon's den, Broca crouched in the shadow of a boulder.

Spying the dragon in the cave, Serf cast aside the staff of hazel wood. Raising both arms to heaven, he began to preach.

The dragon spied Serf and thought: *Dinner!* It lurched to its feet and lumbered out of the cave.

Seeing the size of the beast, Serf's spirit quailed. Truly, the Kinnoull Dragon *was* enormous. But, bravely, he requested that the dragon cease its naughty deeds and help people instead.

The dragon burped, belching flames.

The flames singed Serf's eyebrows and beard.

Serf trembled, but stood his ground, thinking: *I've upset this dragon by being too harsh. I'll chant a prayer. That's sure to soothe its mind.*

As an odd wailing echoed in the air, the dragon took a giant step forward. It bent its forelegs in front of Serf, ready to gobble him whole.

"Look!" cried Serf. "The wild beast kneels to pray with me!"

Roars of approval came from the villagers further down the hill.

Encouraged, Serf gestured to the dragon to lie flat upon the earth.

The dragon put its face against Serf's and opened its jaws.

At that moment it struck Serf that the dragon might *not* be preparing to join him in prayer.

He shut his eyes and commended himself to God.

To Broca, the dragon's intention was obvious. She stood up to yell a warning.

And gasped.

The dragon was so low she had a full view of its head. Between its ears was a patch of bald skin where no scales grew.

Within every living creature is... a soft spot.

Broca dashed out from her hiding place, grabbed the staff, clobbered the dragon on the top of its skull and ducked back behind the boulder.

The beast keeled over at the feet of the holy man.

Serf cautiously opened one eye... and then the other.

"Kindly words and prayer have overwhelmed the beast," Serf stated with complete conviction.

"You have triumphed!" Broca announced, helping him to his feet.

"The dragon is defeated!" Serf proclaimed in a loud voice.

"The dragon is defeated! The dragon is defeated!" the villagers shouted. They had been too far away to see exactly what happened, but now streamed up the hill. Hoisting Serf onto their shoulders, they carried him with shouts of praise to the village.

Meanwhile, the dragon staggered to its feet and returned to its cave for a long rest.

And ever after that, the fearsome beast grazed quietly in the meadows bordering the forest.

So, perhaps the words falling from the lips of the holy man *did* soothe the spirit of the dragon – who can tell?

Or maybe the mighty whack that Broca the woodcutter's daughter gave the dragon's skull made it decide to live peaceably in the cave on the Hill of Kinnoull.

In the village of Dunning, Scotland, there is a church dedicated to St Serf. A few miles away is Kinnoull Hill Woodland Park, where, according to legend, the dragon once roamed. There is a cave there which to this day is known as 'the Dragon's Den'.

The Dragon Apep Fights the Sun God Ra

In the art and symbols of ancient Egypt there are images of Apep, the most famous Egyptian dragon – sometimes shown with the body of a serpent and the head of a crocodile. Apep was the Dragon of Death and Lord of Chaos, and the sworn enemy of Ra the Sun God and Lord of Light.

This story is developed from one of the tales told by the guide-custodians of the ancient tombs and temples along the River Nile.

Apep: **Ah**-pep   Tutankhamun: Tu-tan-**kah**-mun

Each day, from early morning to late evening, Ra, the Sun God, travels across the vast arc of the sky. Rising in the east, the blazing ball of fire bestows light and warmth upon us in the Upperworld.

When Ra descends into the west, sunlight begins to fade. Afternoon shadows lengthen over the land – cold, dense shadows, cast by the head and body of the serpent-dragon Apep, Lord of Chaos and Dragon of Death, who lurks on the western horizon.

The hours from evening until morning are a dangerous time for Ra. The Sun God travels by barge back from the west to the east through the waterways of the Underworld, where there is little light. For these journeys Ra takes on the body of a human with the head of a ram, and places his golden Solar Disc upon his head.

Apep, the Dragon of Death, lives in the Underworld. Although he has never yet succeeded, he has vowed to stop Ra bringing dawn to the eastern horizon. As Lord of Chaos, Apep seeks to wreak havoc upon the Upperworld. Slithering and hissing, he tries to attack Ra and swallow the Solar Disc – to plunge all of us above into eternal darkness.

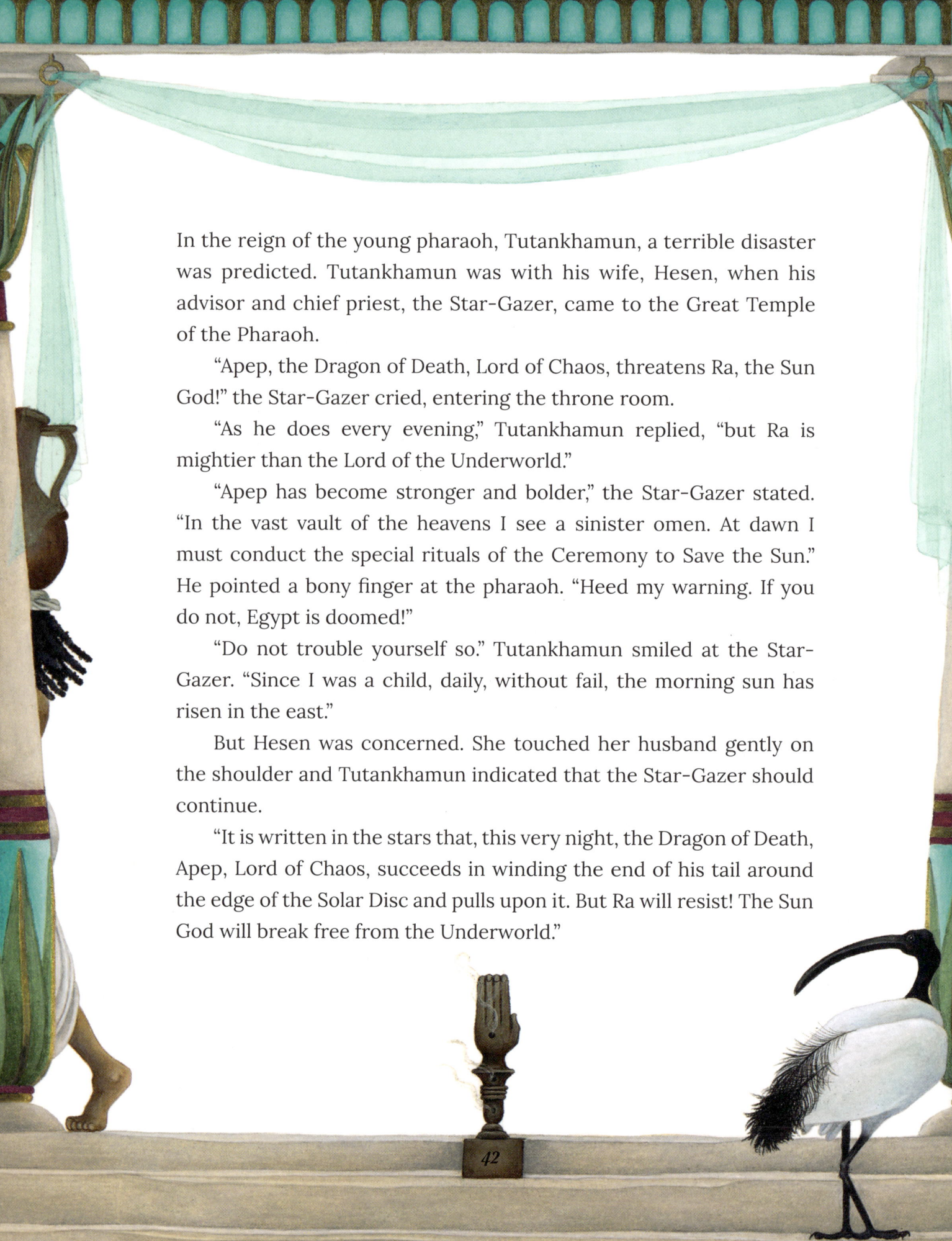

In the reign of the young pharaoh, Tutankhamun, a terrible disaster was predicted. Tutankhamun was with his wife, Hesen, when his advisor and chief priest, the Star-Gazer, came to the Great Temple of the Pharaoh.

"Apep, the Dragon of Death, Lord of Chaos, threatens Ra, the Sun God!" the Star-Gazer cried, entering the throne room.

"As he does every evening," Tutankhamun replied, "but Ra is mightier than the Lord of the Underworld."

"Apep has become stronger and bolder," the Star-Gazer stated. "In the vast vault of the heavens I see a sinister omen. At dawn I must conduct the special rituals of the Ceremony to Save the Sun." He pointed a bony finger at the pharaoh. "Heed my warning. If you do not, Egypt is doomed!"

"Do not trouble yourself so." Tutankhamun smiled at the Star-Gazer. "Since I was a child, daily, without fail, the morning sun has risen in the east."

But Hesen was concerned. She touched her husband gently on the shoulder and Tutankhamun indicated that the Star-Gazer should continue.

"It is written in the stars that, this very night, the Dragon of Death, Apep, Lord of Chaos, succeeds in winding the end of his tail around the edge of the Solar Disc and pulls upon it. But Ra will resist! The Sun God will break free from the Underworld."

"And, as I thought, all will be well." Tutankhamun's tone was reassuring.

"No! Although Ra gains height, Apep's tail will keep its grip on the Solar Disc, and thus he follows Ra into the sky! Fighting for his light and his life, Ra will travel upwards, except…" the Star-Gazer began to wail, "…tomorrow, above our heads we shall witness the last tremendous battle – Apep will swallow the sun!"

Despite his youth, Tutankhamun was a good pharaoh and wanted to protect his people if they might really be threatened by the Dragon of Death. In this he was helped by Hesen, who suggested that instead of holding the Ceremony to Save the Sun inside the Great Temple, the Star-Gazer should perform it in the open air.

"That way Ra may look down and, beholding the pharaoh, gain strength from his support," she explained. "Egypt will see that my husband is not frightened and know that whatever may befall us, we have a true leader."

Tutankhamun, who held his wife in high regard, agreed.

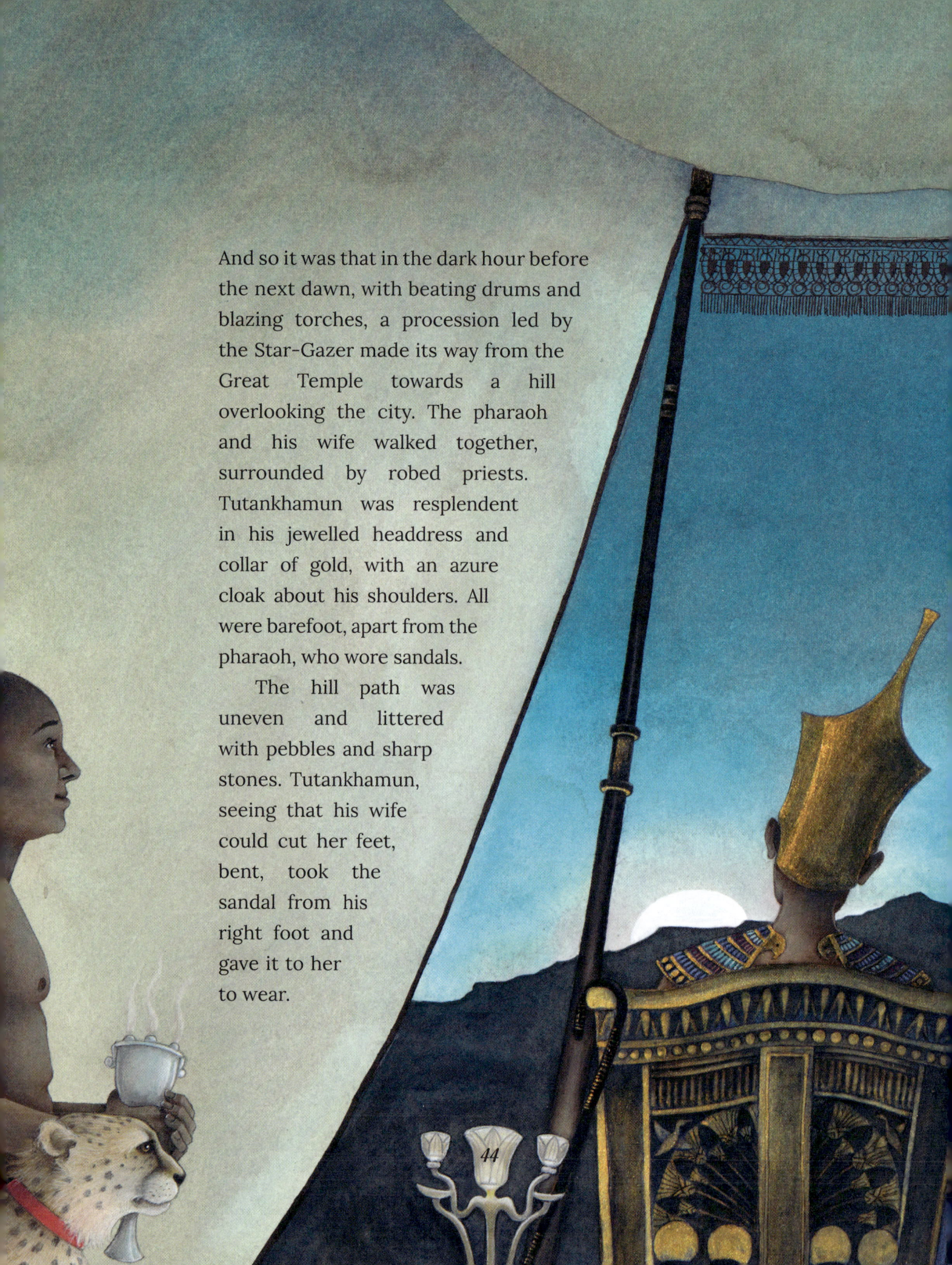

And so it was that in the dark hour before the next dawn, with beating drums and blazing torches, a procession led by the Star-Gazer made its way from the Great Temple towards a hill overlooking the city. The pharaoh and his wife walked together, surrounded by robed priests. Tutankhamun was resplendent in his jewelled headdress and collar of gold, with an azure cloak about his shoulders. All were barefoot, apart from the pharaoh, who wore sandals.

The hill path was uneven and littered with pebbles and sharp stones. Tutankhamun, seeing that his wife could cut her feet, bent, took the sandal from his right foot and gave it to her to wear.

"As we share our love, so do we share what we have," he told her.

On they went to the summit, where ointment, incense and braziers of coal were arranged. The pharaoh's scrolled chair was placed facing east.

The news of the Star-Gazer's prophecy had spread rapidly. People gathered to gaze up at the hill in hope that their pharaoh would save them — for what chance had puny humans once Apep, the Dragon of Death, ruled the land?

The grey glimmer of pre-dawn lanced across the rim of the world and a sigh of relief came from their lips.

The Star-Gazer was wrong!

The sun edged above the horizon, the top half softly beaming amid a hazy cloud. The middle of the Solar Disc, banishing the gloom, was greeted with a babble of voices.

When the full orb was revealed, there was the sound of happy singing. Until...

"The Dragon of Death!" the Star-Gazer shrieked. "Apep's tail!"

The dawn haze had not dispersed. Increasing in thickness, it trailed around Ra. Cloaking himself in streams of mist, Apep followed Ra into the sky. The sun rose higher as Ra travelled onwards. Suddenly Apep pounced!

"Aieee!" The crowds in the valley flung themselves to the ground in terror. "The jaws of the dragon are closing round Ra. Apep is eating the sun!" Lamenting and moaning, they wept and tore at their hair and clothes.

And it was true. By stages, the Solar Disk was disappearing. The dragon was gulping huge chunks of it.

The Star-Gazer and the priests were motionless, frozen in fear.

"Perform the Ceremony to Save the Sun!" Tutankhamun commanded them.

The priests stirred themselves and hurried to obey, murmuring chants and scattering incense into the hot coals. With trembling hands, the Star-Gazer came forward to anoint the pharaoh by rubbing sacred oil upon his forehead.

"Make peace with the victor," he advised. "Prostrate yourself and ask mercy from Apep."

"I will not," replied Tutankhamun. "My subjects could panic if they saw their pharaoh was afraid."

In truth, Tutankhamun *was* afraid, but knew that he must not show it.

"It is wiser to submit," the Star-Gazer insisted.

Again, Tutankhamun refused to bow his head.

A third time did the Star-Gazer beg Tutankhamun to surrender to the rule of the Dragon of Death.

"I am Pharaoh of Egypt," Tutankhamen spoke proudly, "and I will not allow my country to live in eternal darkness."

Then Tutankhamun threw off his cloak so that everyone was aware that he would not submit.

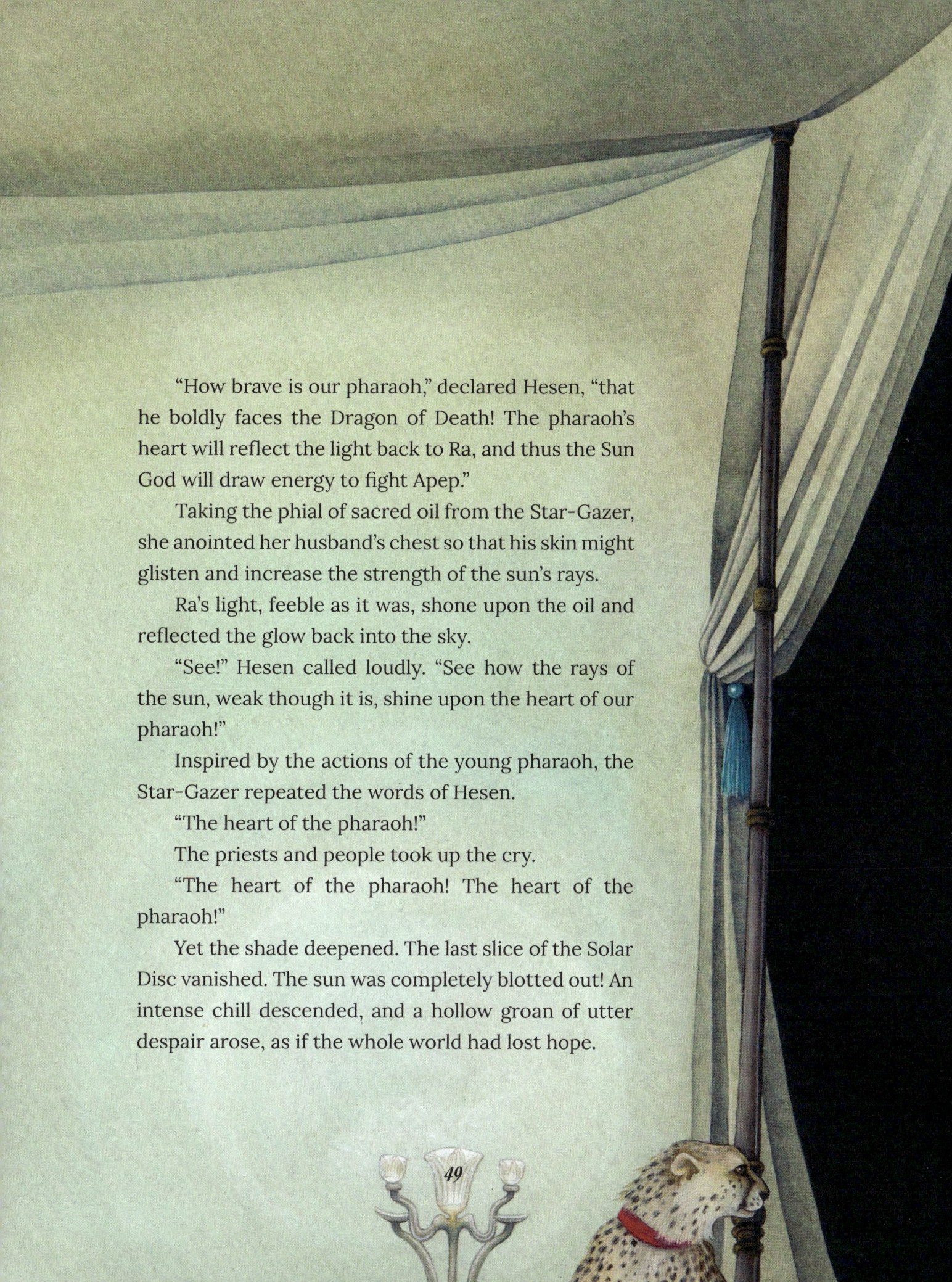

"How brave is our pharaoh," declared Hesen, "that he boldly faces the Dragon of Death! The pharaoh's heart will reflect the light back to Ra, and thus the Sun God will draw energy to fight Apep."

Taking the phial of sacred oil from the Star-Gazer, she anointed her husband's chest so that his skin might glisten and increase the strength of the sun's rays.

Ra's light, feeble as it was, shone upon the oil and reflected the glow back into the sky.

"See!" Hesen called loudly. "See how the rays of the sun, weak though it is, shine upon the heart of our pharaoh!"

Inspired by the actions of the young pharaoh, the Star-Gazer repeated the words of Hesen.

"The heart of the pharaoh!"

The priests and people took up the cry.

"The heart of the pharaoh! The heart of the pharaoh!"

Yet the shade deepened. The last slice of the Solar Disc vanished. The sun was completely blotted out! An intense chill descended, and a hollow groan of utter despair arose, as if the whole world had lost hope.

"Stop!"

It was Tutankhamun himself who shouted now, his voice like rolling thunder, his words carried to the four winds, to the Nile, and the far mountains from whence the river flowed – and beyond them to the furthest lands and oceans of the Earth.

"Stop!" The young pharaoh spoke firmly. "I command thee Apep, Dragon of Death, Lord of Chaos, to release the Sun God and depart from hence."

And Ra, the Sun God, hearing Pharaoh Tutankhamun and seeing the glint of light, sensed a whisper of warmth far beneath. Ra drew this energy into himself, and he pushed against the dragon. The Sun God turned his fearsome gaze upon Apep. In the glare of Ra's light, the jaws of the Dragon of Death weakened. Apep's grip slackened, and Ra began to slip out from the grasp of the crocodile teeth.

A gasp from a thousand throats. A faint cheer welcomed the slimmest sliver of light as the circle of the Solar Disc re-emerged.

The pharaoh, his wife, the Star-Gazer and the priests watched the dark shadow of Apep slide away.

And the Dragon of Death slunk back to the Underworld.

A roar of relief and joy and triumph! Beams of golden light bathed the earth as Ra at the zenith appeared high in the sky once more, bringing warmth and wonderment to the world.

And there were celebrations in Egypt on that day and many days after.

In today's world, too, from time to time, the sun is obscured in the daytime sky because there is a solar eclipse. We understand it differently to the battle Tutankhamun saw between Ra, the Sun God, and Apep, the Dragon of Death.

In 1922, the burial place of Tutankhamun was discovered in the Valley of the Kings in Egypt. Inside the tomb was a special chair. Painted on the back is an image of Hesen, the wife of Tutankhamun, anointing his chest.

Hesen is depicted in this image wearing only one sandal on her right foot and Tutankhamun is only wearing one sandal on his left foot. This is understood as a sign of great affection between two people.

Smok, the Seven-Headed Dragon of Krakow

The beautiful city of Krakow is one of the oldest cities in Poland. It grew from a cluster of houses and shops spread out between the River Vistula and a small castle on Wawel Hill. There are many stories about a real Polish princess called Wanda who lived in the castle.

This story has evolved from a tale told in the thirteenth century. Wanda's father, King Krakus, was fighting battles in a distant land when the people came under threat from an awful seven-headed dragon known as Smok.

Krakow: **Kra**-kufh   Wawel Hill: **Vah**-vel Hill

Smok, the seven-headed dragon, was one of the greediest dragons that ever lived in Europe. It arrived in the country now known as Poland and thought that the Wawel Hill, overlooking the River Vistula, would be a convenient place to stay. The little castle on the hill was too small to hold a dragon. However, the cave underneath it was cosy and next to an enormous forest, which promised plenty of hunting.

When the folk in the village below the castle learned that a dragon had made its home in the cave under the hill, they were not too concerned. The forest was big enough to feed any dragon for a lifetime.

Except that this dragon was not only greedy, it was also lazy. Soon Smok tired of hunting in the forest and took to prowling closer to the village, eating cattle and crops and setting fire to farms and houses by blasting red-hot flames from its seven mouths.

The villagers began to worry.

"The growing season is over and the days are shortening," they said. "With no grain in our barns and no cows to milk, we will surely starve."

Princess Wanda, who lived in the castle on Wawel Hill, heard the people talking. As her mother had died years earlier and her father, the king, was away, Wanda realised that she would have to sort the dragon problem herself. She decided to consult the person she knew best.

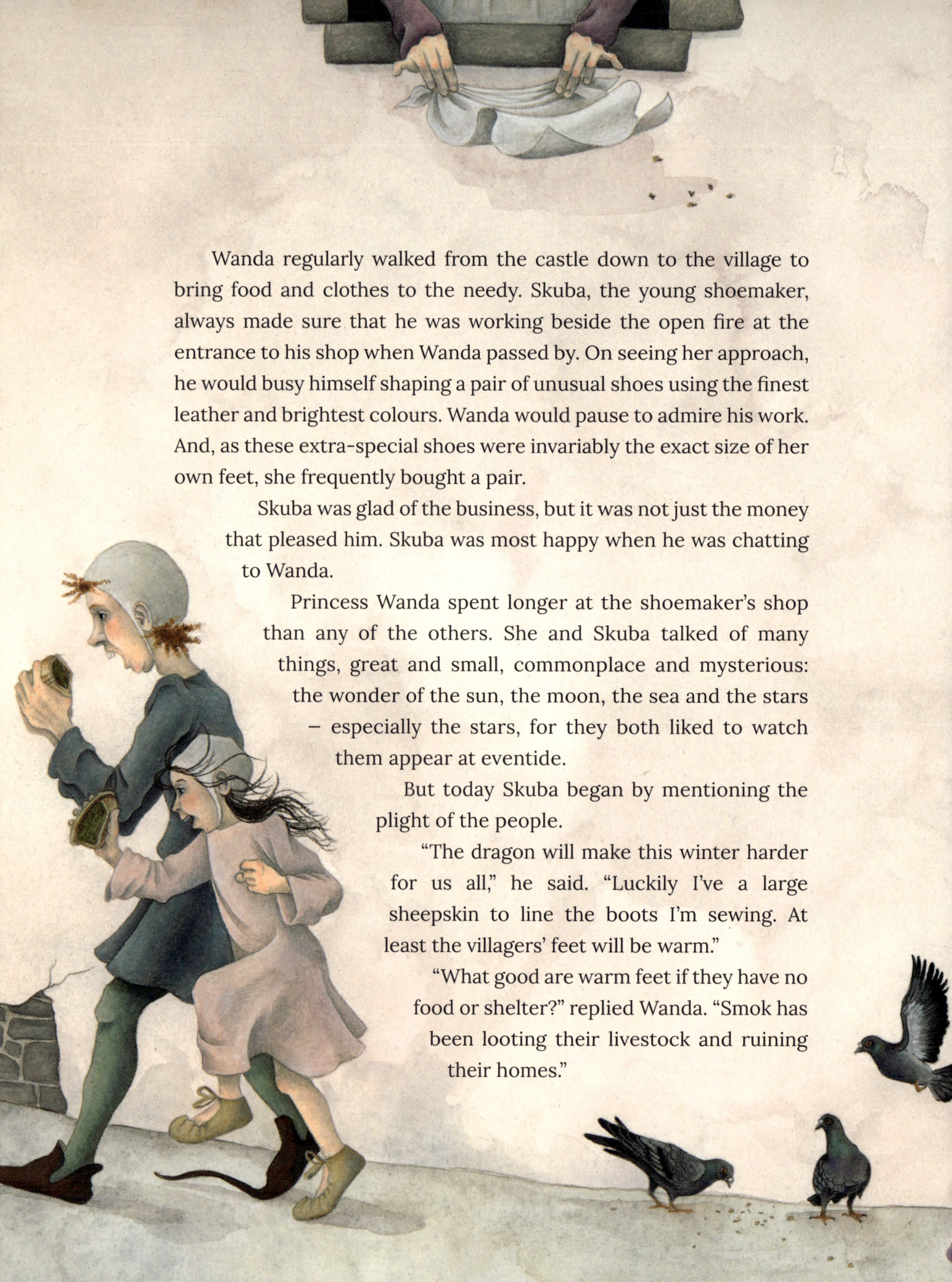

Wanda regularly walked from the castle down to the village to bring food and clothes to the needy. Skuba, the young shoemaker, always made sure that he was working beside the open fire at the entrance to his shop when Wanda passed by. On seeing her approach, he would busy himself shaping a pair of unusual shoes using the finest leather and brightest colours. Wanda would pause to admire his work. And, as these extra-special shoes were invariably the exact size of her own feet, she frequently bought a pair.

Skuba was glad of the business, but it was not just the money that pleased him. Skuba was most happy when he was chatting to Wanda.

Princess Wanda spent longer at the shoemaker's shop than any of the others. She and Skuba talked of many things, great and small, commonplace and mysterious: the wonder of the sun, the moon, the sea and the stars – especially the stars, for they both liked to watch them appear at eventide.

But today Skuba began by mentioning the plight of the people.

"The dragon will make this winter harder for us all," he said. "Luckily I've a large sheepskin to line the boots I'm sewing. At least the villagers' feet will be warm."

"What good are warm feet if they have no food or shelter?" replied Wanda. "Smok has been looting their livestock and ruining their homes."

"This dragon is so idle and greedy," said Skuba, "it wants food nearby, and would eat anything and everything."

Wanda clapped her hands. "I *knew* you would give me an idea." She ran up the hill, back to the castle, to ask the cook to bake a big pie that she could present to Smok. If they supplied the dragon with dinner, hopefully it would be too lazy to go out and steal the villagers' food.

Thereafter, the cook spent each day in the castle kitchen preparing a feast for Smok. And soon each night too, because the more the dragon ate, the more it wanted.

Wanda started to fear that Smok would never be satisfied. In this she was proved right.

One evening, the dragon quickly gobbled its pies, and then looked at her slyly.

"I've a notion to see what human tastes like," it growled. "Instead of a pie, tomorrow you must bring me a villager."

"That's not possible," Wanda said firmly. "In the absence of my father, the king, it is my duty to look after the people. I'm certainly not going to let you start eating them."

"I only want one to taste. I won't ask for another."

"How do I know I can trust you?" Wanda demanded.

"Do as I say," snarled Smok. "Otherwise, I'll destroy the whole village and everyone in it."

Wanda pondered upon this situation as she walked slowly down to the shoemaker's shop.

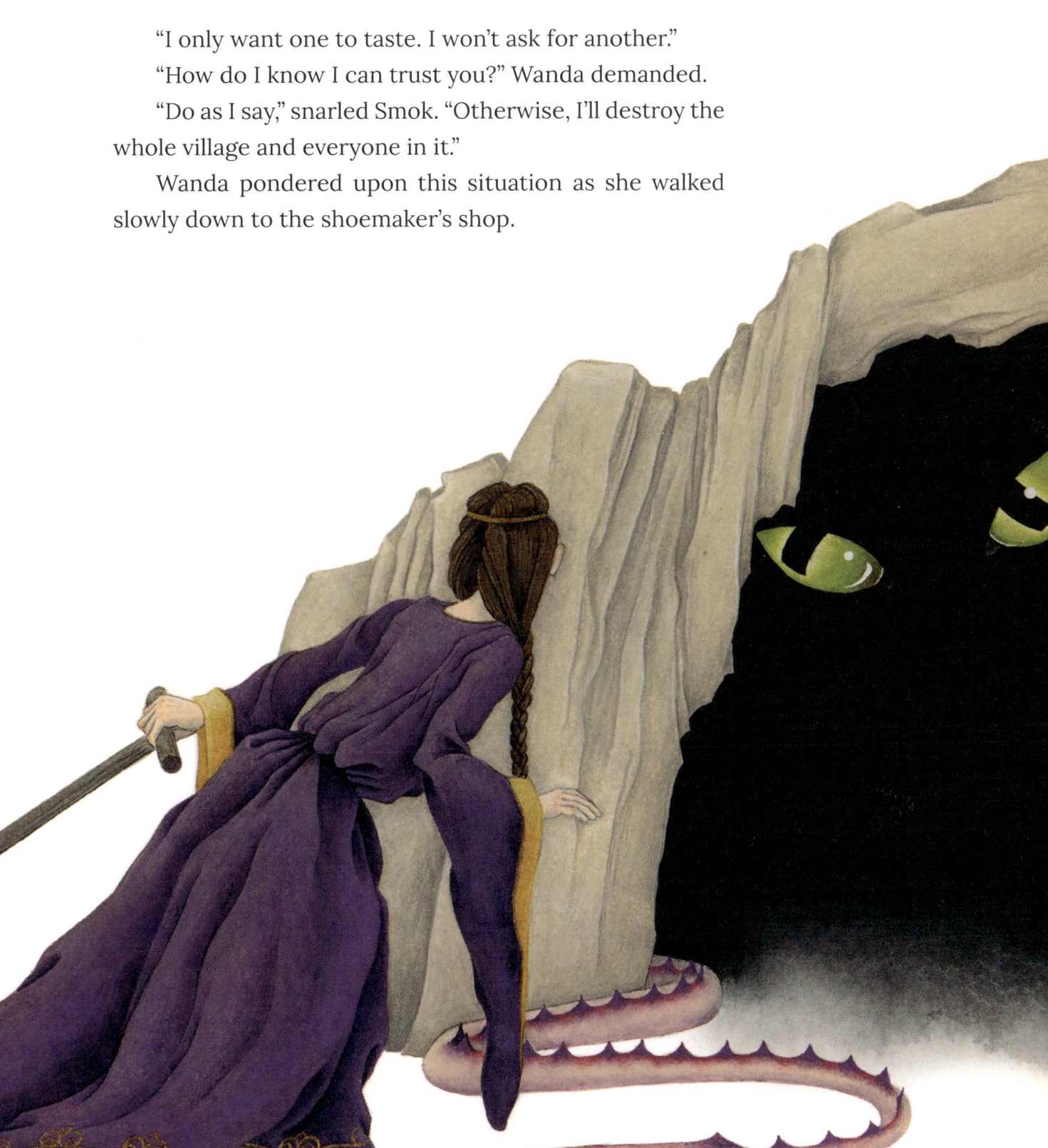

"I've come to say goodbye," she told Skuba, before explaining that she felt it was her duty to offer herself as a snack for Smok. "The dragon says it wants one human to taste."

While Wanda was speaking, Skuba, too, pondered upon the situation. When she had finished, he handed her a pair of tall boots made from bright-yellow leather and lined with woolly sheepskin.

"Oh!" said Wanda, blushing. "Thank you." Then, as Skuba began to buckle on a sword belt, she asked. "What are you doing?"

"I am going to fight the dragon," said Skuba.

"Smok is huge and has seven heads. You will be killed."

"I'd rather be killed than live without seeing your face," said Skuba.

"Aah…" Wanda spoke softly. "I'll miss seeing your face too."

"Having heard that, I can die content," said Skuba.

"Perhaps neither of us need die," Wanda said carefully. She stroked the lining of her new winter boots, and then looked to where the large sheepskin hung on a peg inside the shoemaker's shop. "There might be another way to defeat the dragon. What if Smok is more greedy than smart?"

Wanda walked past the open fire to examine the sheepskin. "A woolly fleece that almost looks like a whole sheep," she murmured. "Are you thinking what I'm thinking?"

Skuba had actually been thinking how brave Wanda was to sacrifice herself to save the village.

"Maybe we could outwit this dragon?" Wanda went on. "This *extremely* greedy and lazy dragon – who, as you yourself said, prefers food brought to it and eats *anything* and *everything*."

A glimmer of understanding came into Skuba's mind as he too examined the sheepskin. "It does almost look like a whole sheep," he agreed.

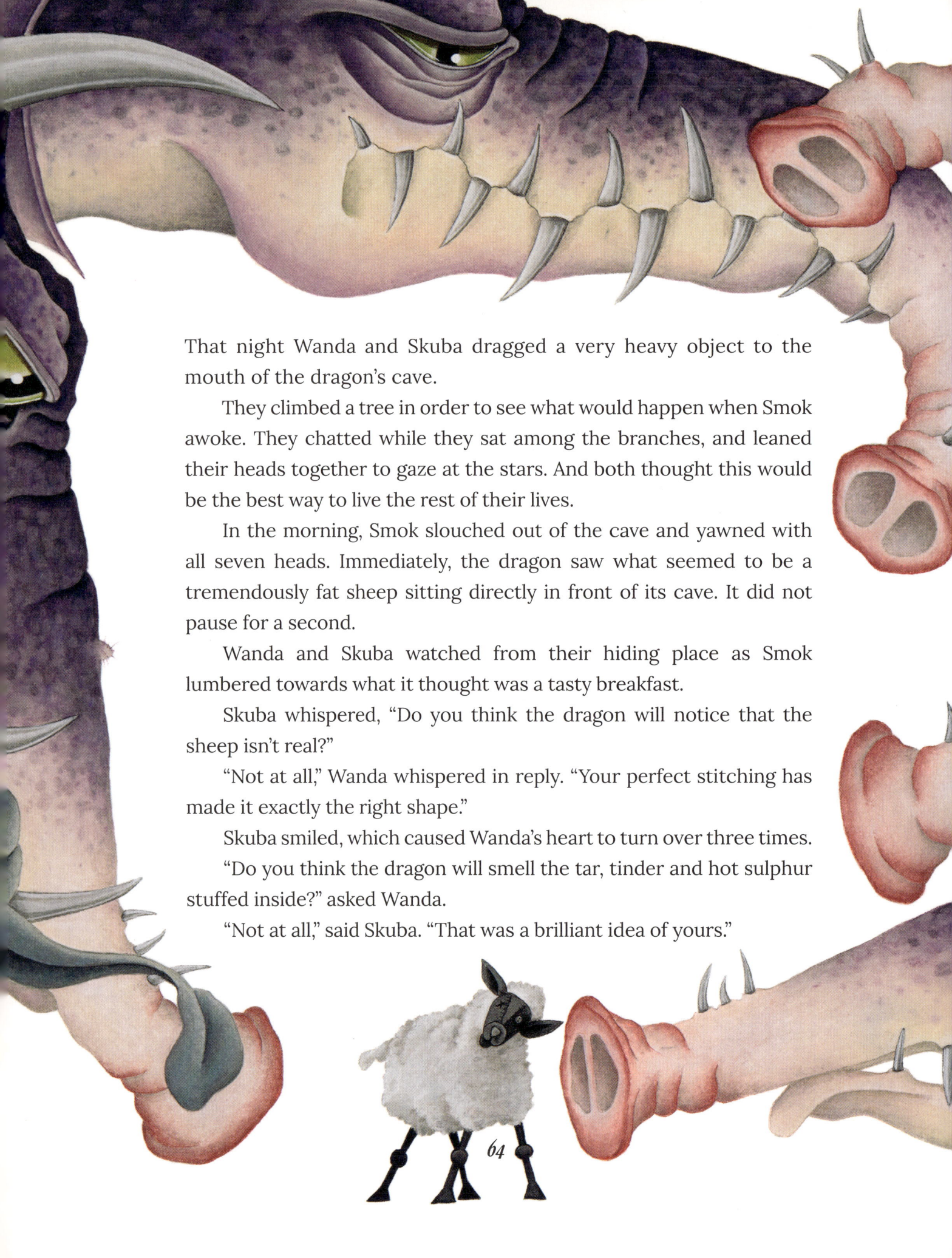

That night Wanda and Skuba dragged a very heavy object to the mouth of the dragon's cave.

They climbed a tree in order to see what would happen when Smok awoke. They chatted while they sat among the branches, and leaned their heads together to gaze at the stars. And both thought this would be the best way to live the rest of their lives.

In the morning, Smok slouched out of the cave and yawned with all seven heads. Immediately, the dragon saw what seemed to be a tremendously fat sheep sitting directly in front of its cave. It did not pause for a second.

Wanda and Skuba watched from their hiding place as Smok lumbered towards what it thought was a tasty breakfast.

Skuba whispered, "Do you think the dragon will notice that the sheep isn't real?"

"Not at all," Wanda whispered in reply. "Your perfect stitching has made it exactly the right shape."

Skuba smiled, which caused Wanda's heart to turn over three times.

"Do you think the dragon will smell the tar, tinder and hot sulphur stuffed inside?" asked Wanda.

"Not at all," said Skuba. "That was a brilliant idea of yours."

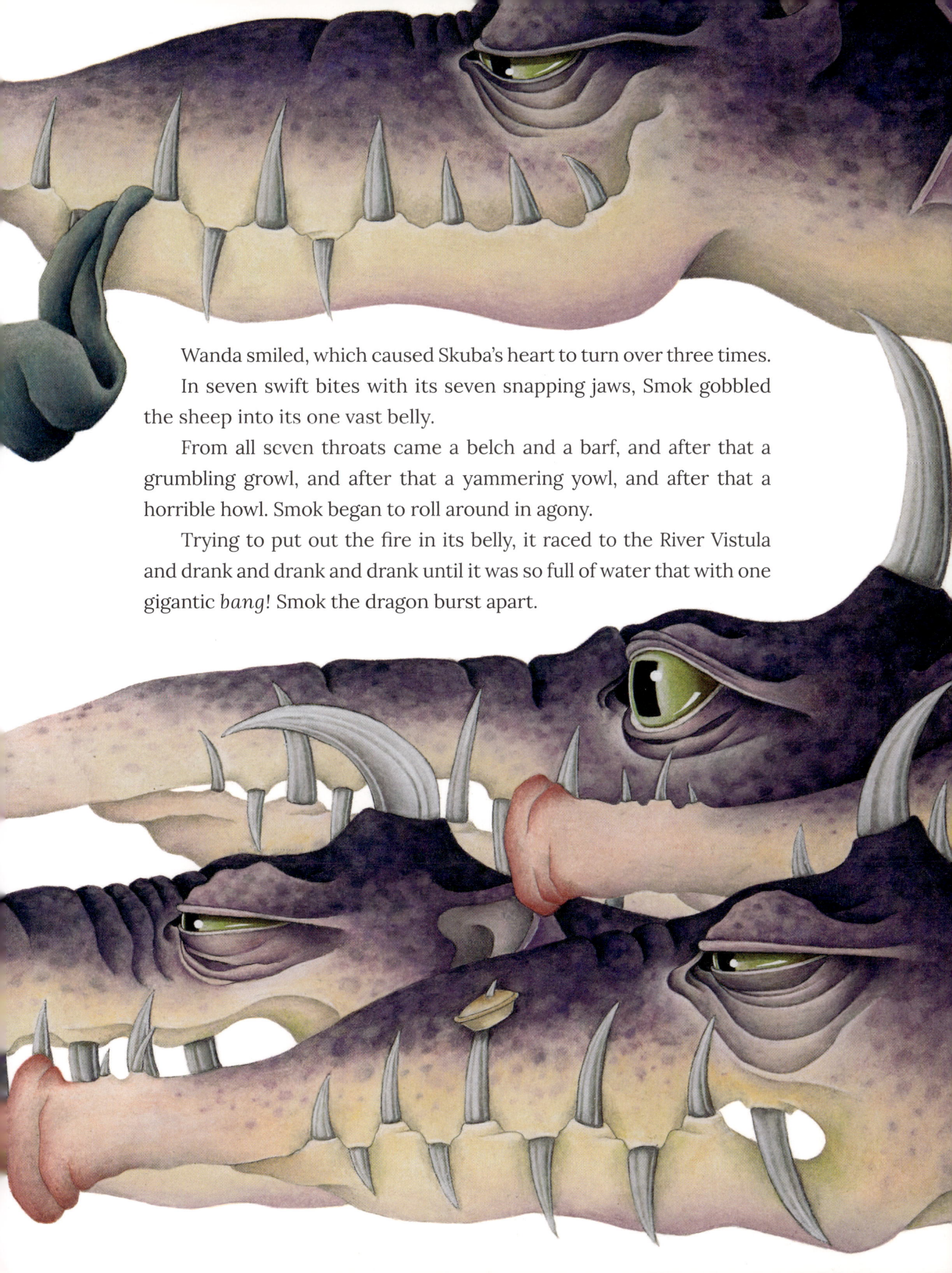

Wanda smiled, which caused Skuba's heart to turn over three times.

In seven swift bites with its seven snapping jaws, Smok gobbled the sheep into its one vast belly.

From all seven throats came a belch and a barf, and after that a grumbling growl, and after that a yammering yowl, and after that a horrible howl. Smok began to roll around in agony.

Trying to put out the fire in its belly, it raced to the River Vistula and drank and drank and drank until it was so full of water that with one gigantic *bang!* Smok the dragon burst apart.

The people of the kingdom were overjoyed and thought that, while the king was away, it would make perfect sense for Princess Wanda and shoemaker Skuba to rule over the country and keep them safe. And Wanda and Skuba happily consented to do just that.

Overlooking the city of Krakow today there is a magnificent castle where Wanda's smaller castle once stood on Wawel Hill.

Near the cave under this hill is a metal sculpture of a seven-headed dragon, reminding passers-by of the story of Smok. Now and then it sends forth a burst of real fire from its jaws.

Kukulkan, the Dragon God of Yucatán

There are many stories from Central America that tell of a dragon called Kukulkan, which is sometimes linked to the Aztec god Quetzalcoatl. The dragon Kukulkan appears in different forms throughout Central America.

This story draws from the legends of the Yucatán Peninsula in Mexico, where Kukulkan is associated with the two days in the year when the sun is directly over the equator, and day and night are of equal length. These are known as the equinoxes; one falls in March, and one in September.

Kukulkan: Koo-kul-**kan**   Quetzalcoatl: Ket-zal-**koh**-ah-tul
Chichen Itza: **Chi**-Chen **Itz**-ah

Long ago, on the evening of the March equinox, at sunset, in a tiny fishing village on the shores of the Yucatán Peninsula in Mexico, twins were born. A boy and a girl.

The girl had brown eyes, and black hair covered her head.

The boy had yellow eyes, and his head was covered with black feathers.

Their father, who was a wise man, said, "We are all in our own way different, and in time we will understand why. We were made for a reason, and each of us has a part to play."

He wrapped his children and laid them gently beside his wife, whereupon the girl reached out her arm to take her brother's hand.

Their mother, who was a wise woman, said, "It is good to see that our son will have someone to watch over him."

And so it was, as the twins grew up, that the girl – who was born first and thus older than the boy – did indeed watch over her brother. She was especially careful of him at the equinoxes in March and September, for those were the times her brother's appearance changed, little by little.

The boy's unusual looks caused the locals to stare and mutter amongst themselves. Sometimes two or three neighbours openly laughed at the boy as the twins went past. When this happened, the girl would turn her head and call back a traditional saying:

"We are all made from the same clay, but not from the same mould!"

With his sister always by his side to support him, the boy managed to smile and ignore the rudeness.

The years went on and the boy's feathers spread down around his neck, changing colour as they increased. By the time he was a young lad, the boy had a splendid collar of feathers, glinting blue and green and gold, shot through with shades of red and purple. His family were proud of him, for he was a gentle soul, and helped his father and sister with their fishing boat and nets.

Although the boy was kind, the neighbours did not repay his kindness, and continued to mock him for his appearance.

The twins got older, and when their parents passed away they remained together, sailing out each morning to catch fish. On the journey back, after the net was drawn in, the boy dived into the sea. Although he often stumbled on land, in water his movements were swift and sure. His sister noticed that her brother's body was becoming more and more snake-like, gliding alongside the boat.

She was not the only one who noticed this. As they walked between the beach and their hut, groups of villagers made hissing noises. Rude remarks followed the pair, and sometimes stones were tossed in their path. The sister was quick to react:

"Those who throw stones at others throw away their own good name at the same time."

Despite the girl's interventions, the gossip increased, even going as far as to suggest that the boy could bring bad luck. If something went wrong – a gusting breeze blowing the roof from a hut, a fisherman returning with few fish – everyone would blame the boy.

"The lad having feathers instead of hair encourages the wind to blow harder in our village," said someone.

"The lad swimming like a serpent in the water frightens the fish. That's why my catch was small," said another.

"Those things are not connected to you," the girl told her brother. "The hut roof was broken and hadn't been mended. The fisherman overslept and so missed the time of the best shoals." She took him by the hand, saying:

"We were made for a reason, and each of us has a part to play."

The twins pretended not to hear the cruel comments, and went quietly about their business, but the behaviour of their neighbours grew threatening.

During July and August the weather was hot and fiery – so too were people's tempers. The villagers held the boy responsible for every trivial mishap – a twisted ankle, a dinner burned. No matter that the person was clambering over slippery rocks, the cooking pot left untended on the fire – somehow, he had caused it to happen. When the girl awoke one night to see an angry crowd with flaming torches marching towards their hut, she knew that they must leave. She hurriedly woke her brother, collected a few possessions, and they escaped into the night.

The twins searched a mile or more along the shoreline to find a sheltered bay and dry cave where they set up home. They didn't go near the village, and sailed their boat further out to sea to fish. The boy's feathers developed into a magnificent mane, framing his face and extending across his shoulders. He became slimmer and longer in the water, and his skin shone silver-scaled. The two of them lived happily together, but sometimes the girl heard the boy whispering to himself in a sad voice:

"*Each of us has a part to play, but what is my part?*"

The hottest months passed. September arrived, and with it, foul weather. The sea was constantly grey and choppy. The day of the equinox approached, when, due to the position of the moon and the sun, the tides are very much greater. Seas around the coast move rapidly and violently, rising higher than normal.

The twins were aware of this, and on the afternoon of the equinox they were returning early from their fishing trip. The boy, as was his custom, swam beside the boat. He had grown stronger and easily sliced through the mounting waves.

Suddenly, a terrified scream echoed in the air.

"Look!" the girl shouted, pointing her finger.

The boy glanced in the direction of the village.

A monstrous tide was racing towards the beach. In front of it, rowing desperately, the fishermen were trying to reach home. On shore the villagers were panicking, gathering their children and fleeing inland. But neither the fishermen nor the villagers could outrun the roaring wave.

This powerful equinox tide would overwhelm them.

In a frozen moment of time the boy saw and understood the danger: the imminent destruction of the whole village. The colossal pounding mountain of water would smash the boats to smithereens, crush the huts, destroy all in its path, sweeping everything and everyone into the sea to be lost forever.

In the same instant he understood something else:

We were made for a reason, and each of us has a part to play.

"And this is *my* part."

The boy lifted his head clear of the water. He stretched, and his whole body melded into an enormously long tail – longer even than the curve of the bay. The multi-coloured feathers of his neck and shoulders spread rapidly in a wide fan and he flew to the village. Wrapping his tail around the boats, he dragged them far up the beach.

And then, fully formed as an immense serpent-dragon, he turned to confront the sea. He laid his whole body along the shoreline as a massive barrier to protect the village.

A second later the incoming tsunami struck with a thunderous shuddering crash. The boy-dragon rocked backwards and might have toppled, except men, women and children rushed to support him. Foam from the great wave frothed over the top of the boy-dragon's tail, but the wall of water was stopped. The sea churned, receded, and gradually ebbed away.

Bruised and battered, the boy-dragon was amazed to see the villagers falling on their knees to beg his forgiveness. He smiled upon them; his heart held no bitterness, for his spirit was now free.

The words his father spoke at his birth had come to pass:

We are all in our own way different, and in time we will understand why.

The people, ashamed of their previous behaviour, praised his goodness and bravery and gave him a special name. Thereafter the boy became known as 'Kukulkan', meaning 'feathered serpent'.

Tradition says that at every equinox in the Yukatán Peninsula, Kukulkan uses his tail to sweep the earth clear. People hear the sound in the wind and take it as a warning that high tides are coming. This means they can prepare, and keep themselves and their homes and boats safe.

    Kukulkan came to be worshipped as a dragon-god. At Chichen Itza there is a temple built in his honour: a pyramid with a special stepped staircase. On the evening of the equinox, the setting sun creates a moving shadow resembling Kukulkan as a long snake slithering slowly down the steps. Thus local people see the dragon-god arriving to help them when they are most in danger.

Jörmungandr, the Dragon Son of Loki

Norse legends and myths from the Scandinavian countries of northern Europe are old, old tales passed down by grandparents, storytellers and poets. Among these tales of gods, giants, humans and a host of other characters is the story of the Serpent-Dragon of the World: Jörmungandr, which is adapted here for children around the world.

Jörmungandr: **Yor**-mun-gander

One of the scariest of the Norse and Viking gods was a serpent-dragon called Jörmungandr who dwelt in the far depths of the sea. His mouth was enormous with long curved teeth, so people stayed away from him. Jörmungandr was content to be alone and only came to the shore when he was summoned by his father.

Jörmungandr's father was Loki, who liked to cause trouble by playing tricks on the other gods. He especially liked to tease mighty Thor, the hammer-wielding warrior. Loki thought it funny when Thor lost his temper, threw his hammer and chased after him, making thunder crash and lightning crackle across the sky.

Every year new challenges were set for the gods, and one year it happened that Thor's task was to empty the Giant Drinking Horn in a single gulp. This horn was set into the wall of Hymir the Giant's castle, which overlooked the sea. While the Giant Drinking Horn was filled with ale, Loki leaned from the castle window and signalled to his son, Jörmungandr.

The horn was vastly long, yet Thor was sure he could drain it with one swallow. Smiling, he put his mouth to the rim and with a great guzzle thought to empty it completely. Wiping his lips, he stood back. To his astonishment, the ale inside still lapped at the top. Once more, Thor placed the horn to his lips and supped the liquid. Once more, the level did not recede. Again and again, Thor tried to drain the horn, but the amount left behind was always the same. On and on Thor drank, until his belly was fit to burst. Finally, the warrior god fell upon the ground in a stupor and had to be carried from the room.

When Thor awoke, Loki taunted him.

"Mighty you may be, Thor, but you are wanting in wit." Loki smirked. "And the opposite of 'in-wit' is 'out-wit', and it is I who have outwitted you today!"

Thor stared at him. "Did you find a way to refill the Giant Drinking Horn?"

"Nay! Not me! But perhaps my son Jörmungandr pierced the narrow end of the Giant Drinking Horn and tipped in water from the sea to constantly refill it as you drank."

Thor, furious at the trick played upon him, began to reach for his hammer, but stopped. He realised that rather than losing his temper, he needed a better way to stop Loki's pranks.

And so Thor decided that, instead trying to catch Loki, he would catch the serpent-dragon Jörmungandr. Then if Loki thought his son was in danger, perhaps he would agree to stop annoying Thor.

Mighty Thor knew that to find Jörmungandr the serpent-dragon he would need a boat and someone to row it. He also knew that fishing in the sea was a favourite sport of Hymir the Giant.

Thor brought Hymir gifts, and asked if he could accompany him on a fishing trip. As Hymir loved to fish, he eagerly agreed, and the two of them left early one morning.

Hymir rowed a little way out to sea, cast his line over the side and quickly caught a small fish.

"You must put your line in the water," the giant told Thor.

"The water here is not deep enough for what I want to catch," Thor replied.

Hymir rowed further out, cast his line over the side and caught a second, medium-sized fish.

"You must put your line in the water," the giant told Thor.

"The water here is not deep enough for what I want to catch," Thor replied.

Hymir rowed even further out, cast his line over the side and caught a third, large fish.

"You must put your line in the water," the giant told Thor.

"The water here is not deep enough for what I want to catch," Thor replied.

"I will venture no further," the giant told Thor. He glanced around nervously. "Where the water is deepest, there be dragons."

Thor snatched the oars from Hymir and rowed furiously to the deepest part of the sea. Then he cast his line over the side of the boat. Almost immediately there was a sharp tug, and the line went taut.

An immense dark shadow loomed alongside them.

"Let us be gone from this place," said Hymir the Giant in a worried voice.

In answer, Thor hauled on his line.

Hymir reached for the oars, intending to row home.

"I'm not leaving until I catch this creature!" cried Thor. He kicked both oars overboard and began to reel in his line.

Gigantic gaping jaws with curved teeth broke the surface. Thor's fishing hook was stuck in the massive mouth!

Muscles bulging, Thor strained and pulled against the heavy weight. Rising up from the depths came the huge hideous head of a serpent-dragon.

"It is Jörmungandr!" Hymir gasped.

"And I have him in my power!" Thor shouted. "I will smack him with my hammer and haul him to shore."

"Let the beast go free," Hymir growled, "for the boat cannot cope with a catch of such strength."

"No!" Face flushed with triumph, Thor yelled his reply. "If I can but bring him to dry land, I'll keep him chained until Loki swears never to bother me again!"

The sea boiled and foamed as Jörmungandr resisted, sending the boat spinning wildly.

"Release the dragon!" begged Hymir. "Release the dragon!"

But Thor was beyond listening to any words of sense. He didn't hear the ominous rumblings of air, water and earth as Jörmungandr twisted his enormous body and lashed his tail. He didn't see the churning seas as Jörmungandr squirmed and writhed. He didn't feel the dreadful shuddering now extending in every direction.

Drawing Jörmungandr ever nearer, with one hand Thor held fast to the fishing line. With the other he pulled his hammer from his belt.

"Stay your hand!" Hymir bellowed, convinced that the boat would capsize and they would be devoured by the monster.

But Thor was not to be thwarted.

The boat rocked. The dragon's violent thrashing now vibrated through all the land, causing catastrophic earthquakes. Mountains heaved up where before there were none, making valleys in between. The land was cleft into parts, creating islands, lakes and fjords.

Seeing this, Hymir feared that the whole world would break apart. The giant grabbed his razor-sharp gutting knife, and in one expert slice, he cut Thor's fishing line.

Thor howled in frustrated rage while Hymir, cupping his big hands like oars, desperately sculled water to bring them back to the shore.

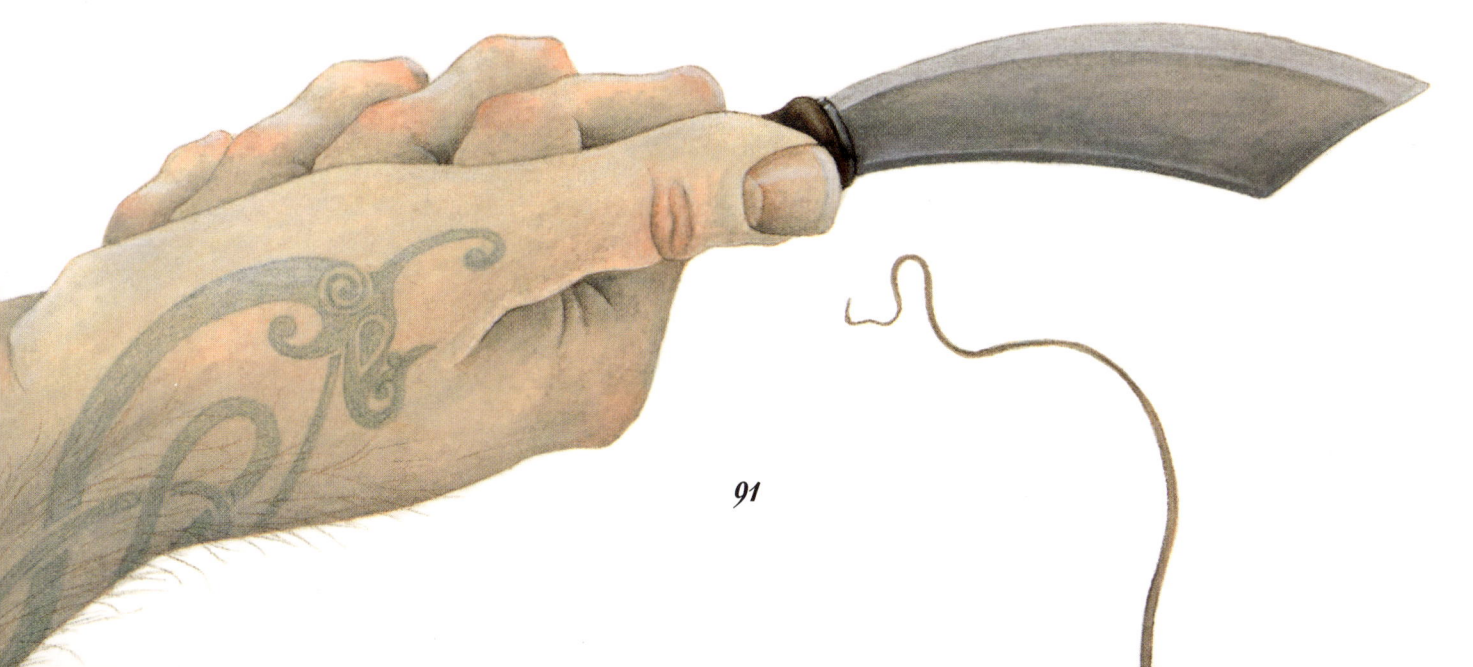

Hymir the Giant returned to his castle determined never to agree to requests from the gods in future – no matter what gifts they gave him.

At first Thor was downcast, but Loki heard what happened and, fearing for the safety of his son, promised not to prank Thor again.

However, Loki does not always keep his promise – which is why we sometimes hear thunder crash and see lightning flash in the sky above.

Jörmungandr settled himself at the very bottom of the deepest part of the sea, where he grew in such strength and length as to encircle the globe.

The story of Jörmungandr and Thor is told in Norse artwork of the time, including in stone carvings that can still be seen, such as the Altuna runestone at Uppland, Sweden.

The Norse myths say that after the struggle with Thor, to ensure that he would not be caught again, Jörmungandr never lay still in one place. Gripping his own tail between his teeth, he undulated his enormous body. Thus the world of humans began to spin.

It is spinning still to this day, and Jörmungandr is known as the Serpent-Dragon of the World.

The Three Dragons of Peterhof Palace

One of the magnificent fountains at Peterhof Palace, near the Russian city of St Petersburg, is a series of waterfalls running down a set of broad black-and-white steps. At the top are figures of three large, fabulously coloured, winged dragons.

The fountain has many legends attached to it. This story is based on one of them.

Milashka: An affectionate term, meaning 'pet'
Raz, Dva, Tri: *Ras, Dvah, Tree*; meaning 'one', 'two', 'three'
 (also 'time, and time again, and a third time').

In the land now known as Russia, centuries before the palace of Peterhof was built, that part of the country was dotted with hills, trees, meadows and streams. Among the people who lived near a wood at the foot of a tall mountain was a girl named Fontan. Every day, while her mama milked the cow, Fontan left their little log cabin to gather the eggs laid by their hens. To prevent the eggs from breaking, Fontan stuffed her basket with straw.

Unusually, spring had brought weeks of dry sunny weather, and Fontan was collecting the hens' eggs in the shade of some trees, when she heard the *tap, tap, tap* of a walking stick on the woodland path behind her. She turned to see an old, old lady, wearing a traditional full-length sarafan dress embroidered in blue, green and red.

"I am starving." The old, old lady's voice quavered as she spoke. "It is three days since I've had a morsel of food in my mouth."

Fontan was a kindly girl and said, "Please come to my house. Even though we are not rich, my mama would be glad to share a meal with you."

"I have to move on," said the old, old lady, "for there is a wealth of work to be done to keep the Earth alive. It is my duty to walk forever, without rest, along the Wild Ways of the World."

"I have no bread here to give you," Fontan said sadly.

"What is in your basket?" the old, old lady asked.

"Some hens' eggs."

"How many?"

Fontan pushed the straw aside to check. "Our hens lay fewer eggs in warm weather," she replied. "There are only three."

"Three," the old, old lady repeated slowly. She looked at the sky, which was clear blue with no cloud in sight. She looked towards the sun, which was already blazing hot. She looked down at the ground, which was dried up and dusty. "Yes, indeed," the old, old lady said finally. "Three eggs should do very well. Thank you."

Fontan hesitated. Despite having generously invited the old, old lady to her house to share a meal, there was not much for them to eat. Her mama would be cross if she gave away their eggs and came home with nothing in her basket.

"Quickly now, because I cannot stop for long in any one place." The old, old lady stretched out her hands for the eggs and Fontan saw her skinny arms. How thin she was!

Fontan's heart moved in pity. Holding out the basket, she offered the old, old lady the three hens' eggs.

The old, old lady grasped them and placed them in the left-hand pocket of her sarafan dress. From the right-hand pocket she took three larger eggs. "As you have given to me," she said, "in the same way must I give to you."

These eggs were unlike any Fontan had ever seen. One was coloured green. One was coloured blue. One was coloured red.

The old, old lady laid them gently in Fontan's basket. "You seem to be a sensible child with a good heart and, when the time comes, you will manage the special task ahead. I entrust these magical eggs to your care." Then, with a *tap, tap, tap* of her walking stick, she shuffled into the woods and disappeared amidst the trees.

Full of excitement, Fontan hurried home.

"Mama! Mama! I met an old, old lady on the woodland path, and she was so hungry that I gave her the eggs our hens had laid."

"*All* of our eggs?" exclaimed Fontan's mama.

"There were only three," Fontan replied. "But, don't worry, Mama. The old, old lady gave me three bigger eggs in return." And she showed her mother the basket.

"*Drakon!*" Fontan's mama whispered in fright.

"These are magic eggs," Fontan chattered on happily, "and I have to take care of them and do a special task."

"What special task?" Her mama whisked the basket from Fontan's hand and laid it on the table to examine the contents. "What did this old, old lady ask you to do?"

"I don't know," Fontan said, realising that she had not been told exactly. "Maybe I'm supposed to use the eggs to bake a special cake?"

Her mama shook her head. "Those are dragon eggs. Poison! We cannot eat them."

"*Dragon* eggs!" Fontan stared at the basket. "Why would the old, old, lady give me three dragon eggs?"

"Was this old, old lady wearing a sarafan dress and leaning on a walking stick?"

"Yes! She was exactly as you say," Fontan answered. "Do you know her?"

"I do not know her," replied Fontan's mama. "Rather, I know *of* her."

"Who is she? What is her name?" Their nearest neighbours were in the village a mile from their house, and few people passed by, so Fontan was curious that her mother could describe someone she had not met.

Fontan's mama sat down and cradled her daughter upon her knee. "My own grandmother called her Baba Yaga, and there are lots of stories about her comings and goings."

"She told me that she could not stay for long in one place," said Fontan, "because she has to walk forever, without rest, along the Wild Ways of the World."

"Never ceasing, Baba Yaga journeys every day, tending the Earth for the benefit of humankind," Fontan's mama continued. "Some say she is the spirit of the Earth itself, but cannot sort its problems. Instead she enables humans to fix the world by giving back in kind what is given to her. You gave her three hens' eggs. Thus she was able to give you three dragon eggs.

"I have heard if she is given a loaf she gives one in return; but her loaf contains seeds that, when planted, grow more grain. She can only help those who help her first. In this way she entrusts the work to a person she believes can do it."

"Baba Yaga said she thought I was a sensible child with a good heart."

"That you are, *milashka*." Fontan's mama kissed her daughter thrice.

"And," Fontan snuggled closer to her mama, "she said that when the time comes, I would manage the task ahead."

"I cannot think what use dragons' eggs are to humankind." Fontan's mama paused, glancing at the table. "When we shut in the hens for the night, it may be safer for us to leave the basket outside."

"A prowling animal would surely eat the eggs!" Fontan protested.

"Baba Yaga gave them to you." Her mama sighed. "Therefore, it is your decision."

Fontan usually listened to her mama's advice, but she recalled the words of the old, old lady: *I entrust these magical eggs to your care.* And so, before going to bed, Fontan placed the basket with the three dragon eggs in front of the stove. As she drifted into sleep, a strange glow lit the darkness of the room: green, blue and red.

Tap. Tap. Tap.

Fontan, dreaming, heard the sound of the walking stick of the old, old lady she had met on the woodland path. And there was Baba Yaga talking to her!

"You must go on a quest to find the most precious thing in the Whole Wide World. Buried deep. Buried high."

Tap. Tap. Tap.

How could something be buried deep *and* buried high? And what could this treasure be? Fontan imagined gold... silver... gemstone crystals...

"Clearer than crystal. Smoother than silver. Greater than gold." Baba Yaga smiled, and her eyes shone like stars in a midnight sky.

Fontan awoke and opened her own eyes. Through her window she saw the stars shining bright in the midnight sky.

Tap. Tap. Tap.

Fontan fancied she could still hear the sound of Baba Yaga's walking stick.

Tap. Tap. Tap.

Fontan sat up in bed. There it was again!

Tap. Tap. Tap.

The noise was coming from the basket by the stove. Fontan jumped out of bed and knelt down beside it.

Tap. Tap. Tap.

A crack zig-zagged across the green egg.

Tap. Tap. Tap.

A crack zig-zagged across the blue egg.

Tap. Tap. Tap.

A crack zig-zagged across the red egg.

Fontan gazed in wonder, unsure what to do next.

Tap. Tap. Tap.

After a moment, to Fontan's astonishment, each of the eggs called out to her.

The green egg cried, "*Raz!*"

The blue egg cried, "*Dva!*"

The red egg cried, "*Tri!*"

The shells shattered. And, with a-crickling and a-crackling, and a-splintering and a-splattering, three little dragons hopped out of their eggs: one green, one blue and one red.

"One! Two! Three!" Fontan clapped her hands in delight. "*Raz! Dva! Tri!*" As she named them, they shook out their tiny wings and went flappity-flip over the edge of the basket onto her lap. There they cuddled together and promptly fell asleep.

For the rest of the night, Fontan watched over the baby dragons. In the morning, and for three weeks afterwards, she and her mama fed them milk from their cow. By that time the dragons were mewing and scratching at the door to go outside. Fontan's mama suggested that she walk them into the foothills of the mountain, taking the cow with her to find grass.

"It has not rained since the last new moon," Mama said, "and our field is shrivelled by the sun. The stream where I get water has dried up. I'll go into the village and fill our bucket from their well."

With Raz, Dva and Tri scampering alongside, Fontan herded the cow towards the nearby mountain. When they reached the foothills, the fried grass was brown. The three dragons scuttled about sniffing the air and then, by yipping and nipping at its heels, guided the cow onto the mountainside.

"Raz! Dva! Tri! Stay on the path!" Fontan ordered.

The little dragons ignored her, and Fontan was obliged to follow them. Maybe Raz, Dva and Tri were the key to the quest Baba Yaga had spoken of? This thought thrilled her. Baba Yaga had said Fontan must seek out the most precious thing on Earth –

"Clearer than crystal. Smoother than silver. Greater than gold." – perhaps it would be made of all three: crystal, silver and gold?

But, although she kept a careful lookout, Fontan spied nothing of worth that day. So absorbed was she in her desire for riches that she barely noticed the withering flowers and the drooping leaves of the trees. Eventually, at a high level, the three dragons led her and the cow to a field of green grass.

Spring faded into summer, and not a drop of rain fell upon the earth. The three dragons grew quickly. Further up the mountain each day Fontan trudged after Raz, Dva and Tri, who never failed to take her and the hungry cow to a patch of fresh grass.

As the weather continued with cloudless skies, the hens stopped laying and the cow gave less milk. Fontan became more and more desperate in her search for the silver, gold and precious stones she believed Baba Yaga wanted her to discover. In addition to bread and cheese for her lunch, she carried a shovel. While the cow grazed, she dug anywhere she thought might be a likely place for hidden jewels. The three dragons scratched between the rocks with their claws. They seemed to be trying to help her. But she found nary a trace of anything precious.

With each passing week of the drought, the digging became more difficult, for the searing heat evaporated all moisture and the earth became harder to break.

One day, on a much higher slope, Fontan paused in her shovelling. Shading her eyes against the glare of the sun, she looked down from the mountain, beyond the foothills, to her home. She saw that the surrounding countryside was scorched barren. Crops were withering in the intense heat, with small fires bursting out here and there in the tinder-dry grass. In the distance she saw her mother returning from her daily trip to the well. By the way she was walking, Fontan could tell that the bucket was almost empty.

"The village well is drying up," Fontan's mama told her that night. "Things are not good with our neighbours. People are becoming ill."

If only I were rich, thought Fontan, *I could buy food for us, and for the whole village.* The next morning she arose at dawn and packed her bag with extra bread and cheese. She wrote a note for Mama to say that she might be gone for more than a day. Then Fontan called on Raz, Dva and Tri and set out for the mountain, determined that she would not return until she had found the treasures she sought.

Stopping at each likely place, Fontan used her shovel to poke and pry into every crevice. Yet, no matter how she tried, she could not loosen a single piece of gravel or grit. Ridge by ridge she clambered on, until by evening she stood at a crag on the highest peak of the mountain. Exhausted, Fontan brushed tears from her eyes, when a sudden breeze from far away seemed to carry the words of Baba Yaga to her ears.

Buried deep and buried high.

She had climbed as high as possible, yet there was nothing here! In despair Fontan flung her shovel against the solid stone.

It struck sharply, and bounced twice more.

Tap! Tap! Tap!

Fontan stared at the rock face. Three cracks had appeared!

She bent to pick up her shovel but Raz, Dva and Tri were there before her. Scraping and tearing with sharp teeth and claws, they expanded the three cracks until, fully widened, they opened up the entrance to a dark cave.

Treasure! thought Fontan, heart thudding in excitement. *Now I will find the most precious thing in the Whole Wide World!*

With Raz, Dva and Tri beside her, she stepped inside.

Raz raised his head. From his jaws flared a flame of palest green. Fontan gasped. Ahead, glittering on the roof, she saw sparkling crystals.

Gemstones!

Dva raised his head. From his jaws flared a grey-blue flame. Fontan gasped. Ahead, glinting on the walls, she saw shining strands.

Silver!

Tri raised his head. From his jaws flared a yellow-red flame. Fontan gasped. Ahead, shimmering on the floor, she saw an odd gleaming.

Gold!

But in that instant the last rays of the setting sun shone through the opening to illuminate the cave from end to end. And Fontan realised that it was only the *colours* of gold, silver and gemstones which were on the walls, roof and floor. What she was *actually* seeing – *Clearer than crystal. Smoother than silver. Greater than gold.* – was truly the most precious thing in the Whole Wide World...

Water.

For three days and three nights Fontan and her three dragons burrowed into the very heart of the mountain. They discovered hidden springs and lakes where rain had gathered over years and years. The three dragons tunnelled further, deeper, to direct the water, like an underground river flowing down to the base of the mountain, and along under the earth to the village.

When all was ready, Fontan returned from inside the mountain to the entrance cave at the top and, still clutching her shovel, climbed down to her home.

"Mama! Mama!" She burst into their house. "We must go to the village at once. I want to show you the most marvellous sight!"

Calling on the people as she went, Fontan arrived at the well in the village.

"There is only a trickle left," her mama told her. And the villagers nodded unhappily in agreement.

Fontan smiled. Lifting her shovel, she struck the side of the well three times.

Tap! Tap! Tap!

With a mighty roar three dragons burst from below the bottom of the well and flew into the sky above the villagers, flashing flames of green, blue and red.

The people screamed. First in fear.

Then in joy.

For close behind Raz, Dva and Tri, a glorious spray of water shot upwards.

Soon everyone's buckets and barrels were filled.

The villagers built a beautiful fountain there at the well, to recycle the water and turn it off and on when needed.

Fontan, seeing nature reviving again, understood that she had indeed found the real treasure of the Earth; and, for the rest of her long life, she tended the fountain carefully, helped by the three dragons, Raz, Dva and Tri.

One of the oldest fountains at Peterhof is the Dragon Hill Cascade: three dragons guard an upper grotto, spewing streams of water from their jaws. No pumps are needed to maintain the stream of this fountain. Could it be that the three dragons are the source of the strong flow...?

Dragons appear in Russian folklore as nasty creatures, often with multiple heads. In many traditional tales they behave very badly indeed, unlike Fontan's three young dragons, Raz, Dva and Tri.

The Dragon of Colchis, Guardian of the Golden Fleece

In ancient Greece many stories were told about mythical creatures, brave heroes and how the gods and goddesses, who lived on Mount Olympus, watched over life on Earth.

The epic myth-poem Argonautica, written in the third century, tells of the adventures of a prince called Jason. This story is a retelling of the part where Jason makes a dangerous journey to regain his father's throne - a quest which will lead him to confront a dreadful serpent-dragon.

Aeetes: Eh-**ee**-teez

Prince Jason was the son of a king in ancient Greece. When he was a child, his uncle, Pelias, murdered Jason's father and made himself king. Jason managed to escape, and when he grew up he decided to meet with Pelias and demand the return of his rightful throne.

On his way to speak to Pelias, while about to cross a river, Jason saw an old lady crouched by the bank.

"I am too feeble to make my way over," she moaned. "If I tried, I would surely drown."

Although he did not want to delay his journey, Jason was of a kindly nature. "Let me carry you," he said, and, lifting the old lady, he waded into the water.

Suddenly the flow of the river increased to a raging torrent and the ground shifted and split apart under Jason's feet. Three times he tripped, crashing to his knees. Three times the old lady was almost torn from his grasp. Struggling to stay upright, it would have been easier for Jason to let her go, but he held on firmly until they reached the opposite side.

Whereupon the old lady leapt nimbly from his arms and stood tall and elegant in front of him. Her features changed, and she revealed herself as Hera, queen of all the gods.

"The immortal gods of Mount Olympus were testing you, Prince Jason," she told him. "We deem your actions those of a good man. I will guide you to regain your throne."

Before leaving, Hera gave Jason an amulet of red clay to wear around his neck. To anyone else it seemed to show the face of an old woman. However, when Jason gazed at it, the features changed to become those of Hera, queen of the gods.

The amulet spoke to him: "Three times you withstood the flood and did not flinch," Jason heard Hera's voice say. "Three times, therefore, you may call upon me to ask a god of Mount Olympus to come to your aid."

Prince Jason was glad, for he sensed that it would be hard to defeat Pelias, who was known to be deceitful and devious.

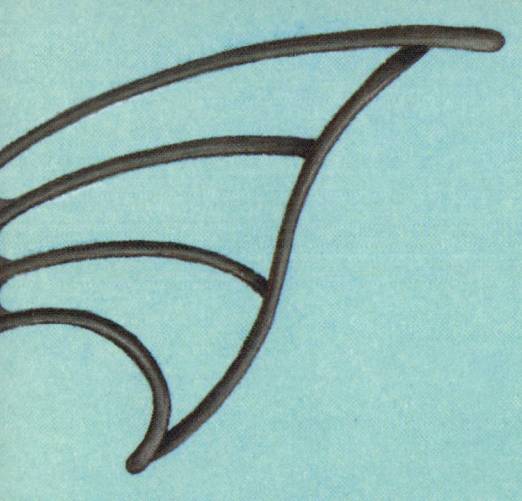

And indeed, when they met, instead of arguing, wily Pelias listened to the young man and agreed that Jason might regain his throne – "but *only* if you can prove that you are fit to be a king," Pelias declared loudly before his whole court. "You, Jason, must sail to the distant land of Colchis and bring home the famous fleece of gold that is guarded by a dreadful serpent-dragon."

This fleece came from a magical ram, whose wool had been turned to glittering gold by the sun god. As treasure, it was worth a vast fortune. More importantly, everyone believed that whoever held the Golden Fleece had the right to be a king.

Jason knew he needed a sturdy ship and a special crew. His ship – the longest ever built – was named the *Argo* and those who went with him on this epic quest became known as the Argonauts. Most were fully armed fighters. But, to entertain the men on their journey, Jason also invited along his friend, the bard Orpheus. When Orpheus played upon his lyre, the very birds of the air ceased their singing to pay attention. His sweet music soothed strife and calmed worry, until the listener became drowsy unto sleep.

The king of Colchis was called Aeetes. As you may imagine, Aeetes was alarmed when the Argonauts moored their ship in his harbour. He mounted his war chariot, assembled his nobles and soldiers, and rode to meet the strangers.

Prince Jason explained that he desired nothing but his own kingdom and had great need of the Golden Fleece.

King Aeetes wanted to keep the Golden Fleece, and keep his army and navy undamaged. He pretended that he would treat Jason's request fairly.

"If we do battle," said Aeetes, "the Argonauts will surely lose. Strong as you are, we are many and you are few. Yet I would not have my country laid to waste and strewn with corpses on both sides. Nominate a champion to be put to the test by me. Your quest will stand or fall upon the result."

The test was to tame two fire-breathing bulls and yoke them to plough a rocky field. And then to sow in the field a dozen serpent's teeth, from each of which, in an instant, would spring a heavily armed warrior. All of these twelve warriors were to be struck down. The three tasks were to be done that day, or else Jason and his crew must leave at once and never return to Colchis.

Every Argonaut volunteered to undertake the test, but Prince Jason stated that he would be the one to go forward.

Before he spoke out, Jason recalled Hera's voice in his head, and he clasped the red amulet in his hand:

"Hera," he whispered, "this first time I beg you, send a god to assist me as you promised when I did carry thee through the raging torrent."

The features on the amulet changed, and Hera smiled upon Jason.

Now, among those who lived with King Aeetes was his gifted daughter, Medea. Hera was aware that Medea was a clever sorceress, and would be able to aid Jason. And so Hera summoned the goddess of love, Aphrodite, to cause Medea to fall in love with Jason. The goddess of love sent a tiny arrow, a single sliver of steel, to lodge in Medea's heart.

Thus when Medea saw Prince Jason – clad in saffron robe with sword and shield in hand – step up to take the test, she was filled with love for him.

Swiftly Medea concocted a magic potion which protected skin from any scratch and bones from any break. She pressed the tiny bottle into Jason's hand and urged him to drink. And Jason, seeing the love-light in Medea's eyes, and believing that she wished him well, swallowed it immediately.

Therefore, the fiery breath of the bulls did not scorch Jason, nor did their thrusting horns pierce him, nor any of the twelve warriors born of the serpent's teeth defeat him. After battling for hours, Jason completed the three tasks set by King Aeetes and asked for his reward of the Golden Fleece.

King Aeetes was furious, but overcame his rage enough to address Jason:

"The bell of the night-watch is sounding and the day is darkening. Your toil has made you weary. Even with my directions you would be unable to collect your prize, for it lies in a secret grove guarded by the dreaded Dragon of Colchis. Take your crew to the harbour and be at rest. Tomorrow, at noon, I will bring you the Golden Fleece."

Then Aeetes privately told his army commander to prepare to attack and slay the Argonauts in the early morning when they would lie sleeping and unarmed on their ship.

Medea overheard this. She slipped out of the palace and went to tell Prince Jason of her father's treachery. Jason looked lovingly at Medea and asked her to accompany him home. So happy was Medea that she offered to show Jason the path to the secret grove.

By strange and winding ways Medea led Jason, until amid the pitch-black forest a shimmering light appeared. At first Jason thought it was the rising sun, but ahead was a clearing where grew a huge three-trunked oak tree. Draped over the branches of the oak, the burnished wool of the Golden Fleece shone out in dazzling glory.

Jason halted in awe.

Then, excited at seeing his long-sought prize within his grasp, Jason raced forwards. In the shadows he didn't notice what lay at the foot of the triple-trunked oak. He had forgotten about the guardian of the secret grove: the dreaded Dragon of Colchis.

Trampling on what he thought were thick tree roots, Prince Jason reached for the Golden Fleece. He stretched out his arms. Soon he would be a rightful king!

Jason's fingers brushed the edge of the wondrous Fleece. And at that moment the earth shuddered beneath his feet.

"The dragon!" Medea cried. "The dragon is awake!"

Jason took a pace away and beheld a sight that chilled his blood.

Writhing about his ankles was the immense body of the serpent-dragon. He leapt back. Too late! The sinewy tail had snaked around his legs. Jason was trapped!

The dragon tightened its grip. Jason drew his sword and slashed at the monster. The dragon's coils looped higher, to Jason's shins... his thighs... crushing ever tighter. Jason hacked desperately as he felt the power draining from his legs. The dragon's coils were at his waist! Using his two hands, Jason raised his sword and, with supreme effort, plunged the blade deep into the dragon's scaly hide. The beast loosened its coils and Jason sprang free.

But the creature was wide awake now and restless, swishing to and fro, its body longer than the *Argo* from stem to stern. Swirling like running ropes, the dragon uncurled, while the earth beneath it tumbled open, revealing gaping holes oozing thick yellow slime.

Jason paused. The safety of his ship beckoned him. But to have come so far and go home empty-handed was too much to bear.

Slithering along the ground, the dragon wound itself round the three trunks of the oak tree. Woven among bark and branches, it merged in the darkness, so that tree and dragon were as one.

But the shining Fleece still tempted Jason and, bending low, he crept on stealthily.

A hiss rent the air. Another and another vibrated through the grove.

A blazing light shone from the dragon's eyes. The twin beams lit up the ghastly face, seeking its prey. Fangs extended and forked tongue flickering, the dragon strained its neck to strike. Jason dodged, but the glittering eyes searched this way and that relentlessly, raking the gloom, while Jason, trembling, hesitated.

Prince Jason steadied his nerve. In those days it was considered dishonourable for a hero to refuse to confront the enemy. Jason spoke to Medea. "In fair fight I will engage the Dragon of Colchis."

"Wait! Wait!" Medea placed her hand on his arm.

"Your potion will save me," Jason reassured her. "This dragon cannot harm me. Neither burn nor bruise nor broken bone will I suffer."

"But, see!" Medea pointed at the triple-trunked oak. "Death approaches! A death against which there is no protection!"

Rolling towards them was a seething fog of greenish smoke, and past them deer and rabbit and other woodland creatures came, fleeing in terror. But as the noxious fumes overtook the animals, they collapsed.

"The dragon is blowing out a poison," Medea warned. "The potion I gave you will not keep you alive if you inhale its toxic breath."

The angrier the dragon became, the thicker flowed the foul air.

"I must have the Fleece! Or die in the attempt." Jason strode on.

"Let me go in your place!" Medea ran past him. "I will sacrifice myself for you." Clawing the air and gasping for breath, she swayed, and would have fallen had Jason not caught her.

Coughing and stumbling himself, Jason gathered Medea up. With bitter disappointment he realised the fog would engulf them both. They had to retreat.

Jason carried Medea to the ship and found a place for her to rest. In despair and anger his crew argued amongst themselves as to what to do next while they awaited Jason's command.

Before he spoke out, Jason recalled Hera's voice in his head, and he clasped the red amulet in his hand:

"Hera," he whispered, "this second time I beg you, send a god to assist me as you promised when I did carry thee through the raging torrent."

The features on the amulet changed, and Hera smiled upon Jason.

And so Hera summoned the goddess of wisdom, Athena, who touched Jason's forehead lightly to open the ears and eyes of his mind. For to properly see and hear is the foundation of wisdom.

Jason saw Orpheus begin to strum upon his lyre. And Jason heard the music and saw its effect – how the Argonauts began to talk more pleasantly, think more clearly.

He tapped his friend on the shoulder. "Please Orpheus, will you come with me to the sacred grove and bring your lyre?"

Orpheus readily agreed. Jason bade the crew to be ready to cast off at a moment's notice, and he returned with the bard to face the Dragon of Colchis.

Never did a musician play such as Orpheus did that night. The notes wafting through the air entered the soul of the Dragon of Colchis and its body relaxed. The poisonous mist thinned and drifted. The intense light in its eyes dimmed. Slowly, it sank down. The music of Orpheus worked its charm.

And the dreaded Dragon of Colchis fell asleep.

Stepping warily around the gleaming fangs, Jason lifted the Fleece from where it hung, and placed it across his shoulders like a heavy golden cloak.

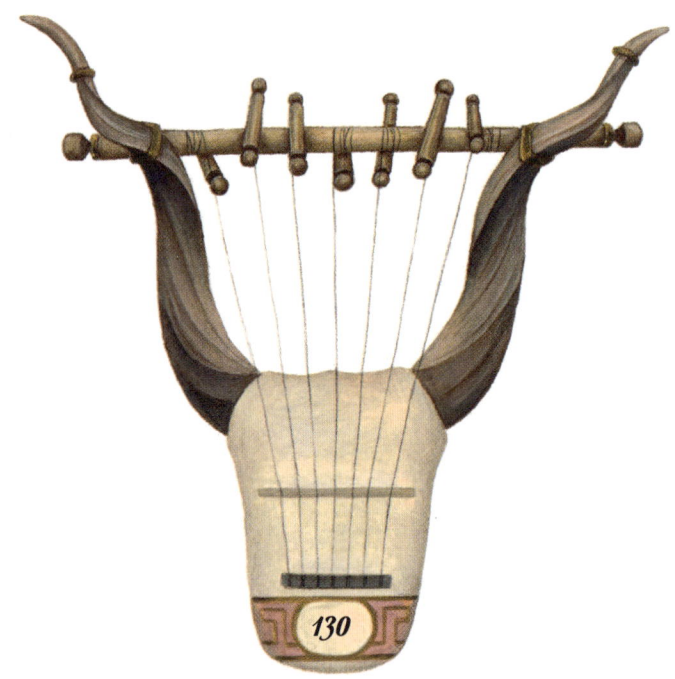

Sunbeams were lighting the sky as Jason and Orpheus ran to the harbour, calling upon the crew.

The war chariot of King Aeetes came racing from the palace, an army of a thousand behind him with bows and arrows and sharpened spears. And a hundred sailors of the king's navy were scrambling to launch their ships.

"Do we defend ourselves on land or water?" the Argonauts asked Jason, for it was clear that they would be blocked from leaving the harbour and must choose where to fight and die.

Before he spoke out, Jason again recalled Hera's voice in his head, and he clasped the red amulet in his hand:

"Hera," he whispered, "this third and last time I beg you, send a god to assist me as you promised when I did carry thee through the raging torrent."

The features on the amulet changed, and Hera smiled upon Jason.

And so Hera summoned the god of the sea, Poseidon, to help Prince Jason.

As Jason and Orpheus leapt aboard the *Argo*, Poseidon whirled the harbour water into a rip tide. Rising from the deep, he raised their ship onto the crest of the outgoing current. Then the great god of the seas and oceans blew wind to fill the sails.

The Argonauts plied their oars as the *Argo* rode the roaring wave onwards, taking the Golden Fleece and Jason home to claim his throne.

King Aeetes tore his garments and ordered that the sacred grove be forever enclosed within a high wall of spiked staves.

To this day no one has entered the secret grove to find out if the dreaded Dragon of Colchis still sleeps with its enormous body coiled around the triple-trunked oak tree.

In mythology, dragons are often featured as guardians of fabulous treasure. The treasure of the Golden Fleece, guarded by the dragon of Colchis, is at the heart of one of the most famous Greek legends – a classic story still of interest today.

The Golden Fleece is the wool of a mystical ram that is also honoured in the constellation called Aries, shining forever in the night sky.

Toyotama-hime, Dragon Princess of the Sea

The dragons which appear in the folklore of Japan are often kindly creatures – wise, brave and strong. The symbol of the dragon is linked to the emperors of Japan.

This story is derived from a Japanese folktale about Toyotama-hime, who is a serpent-dragon from the family of the dragon Sea God. Toyotama-hime was able to change shape from her serpent-dragon form, becoming any fish or animal she wished to be, or taking on the form of a human.

Toyotama-hime: Toyo-tama-**hee**-may   Ryūjin: Ri-**yoo**-jeen
Hiko: **Hee**-ko

Toyotama-hime – the Princess Toyotama – was a daughter of the dragon Sea God Ryūjin. Like everyone in her father's undersea kingdom, Toyotama had special shape-changing powers. She was most comfortable in her natural form of a *tatsu* – a scaly skinned serpent-dragon resembling a very long crocodile – yet could become any fish or mammal she wished.

Toyotama was more adventurous than the rest of her dragon family, and often secretly stole away from the magnificent underwater palace where they lived. She wandered the seas around Japan, visiting lagoons and caverns, changing shape to swim with the various creatures who dwelt there. As a salmon Toyotama joined the search for their spawning grounds, as a sardine she moved and twisted within their glittering shoals. Among a pod of whales, she echoed their language as they travelled their ocean routes. She danced with seahorses, and played hide-and-seek with ink squid and octopi.

Leaping with a school of dolphins one day, Toyotama caught sight of Prince Hiko, a descendant of the sun goddess, sitting on a clifftop. She paused to watch him, for the young man seemed to be in distress. Weeks previously, Hiko had borrowed a precious silver fish hook from his brother and managed to lose it in the ocean. This caused a huge argument between them, and Hiko knew that his brother would not speak to him again unless he found the missing fish hook. In sorrow and despair, Hiko cast himself from the cliff, shouting:

"Oh, mighty sun goddess, ancestor of mine, I beg you show me where my brother's fish hook lies!"

Toyotama heard the cry and, fearing for his life, she swam towards Hiko. So as not to alarm him, she altered her shape from dolphin to human form.

Hiko was not too surprised when a gracious young woman appeared beside him in the water, believing that his sun goddess ancestor had sent her to assist him.

"I know the seas around Japan better than anyone," Toyotama told him. "I will go with you until we find what you have lost."

True to her word, Toyotama did help Hiko in his quest. Because they were both descended from gods – Toyotama from the Sea God and Hiko from the sun goddess – they were able to exist quite easily in the water. For three years they searched. However, they hardly noticed the time pass, so happy were they in their own company.

They asked sea urchins and scallops, kisu and karei, crabs and shrimps and anchovies, yet none knew where the missing silver fish hook lay.

After they had enquired in all the seas, they sought their answer from the air. Gull and guillemot, auk and albatross, puffin, petrel and plover could tell them nothing. It was only when they happened upon a kindly clever cormorant, who could dive deep underwater, that they heard of an elderly perch, lurking in a sunken ship, who had a silver fish hook trapped in its mouth.

What delight there was for Toyotama and Hiko now that their quest was done and the fish hook returned safely to its owner! They had not merely found the fish hook; they had also discovered great affection for each other.

As they stood below the clifftop by the shore where they first met, Hiko declared his feelings for Toyotama, saying:

"You have brought peace to my mind, for I am reconciled with my brother. You have brought love to my heart, for I am always happy in your presence."

And Toyotama, gazing into his face, declared her feelings for Hiko, replying:

"You have brought peace to my mind, for I no longer want to wander the seas. You have brought love to my heart, for I am always happy in your presence."

The dragon Sea God Ryūjin agreed to their marriage and, in order not to scare Hiko, ordered that everyone within his underwater kingdom change from their *tatsu* dragon shape to human form. Hiko was charmed by his new home and never saw Toyotama, or any of her family, in their dragon form. With towers of rose-red coral and walls glittering with fish scales, he thought the magnificent palace of Ryūjin a wondrous place to be. Soon Toyotama-hime and Hiko were wedded with grand ceremony and splendour.

Although for a while Hiko was content, after three years he began to pine for his own people and lands. Toyotama was persuaded that they should visit his family on the hard surface of the earth and, sadly, left her father and friends.

They stayed in Hiko's castle on land for three years, whereupon they found out that they were expecting a child. Toyotama wanted to go home for the birth of the baby and live there, so that her child would be brought up with her little cousin, whose name was Tamayori. Hiko wanted her to remain so that the baby would be born in *his* homeland.

He spoke seriously to Toyotama, saying:

"I am your husband and a descendant of the sun goddess. It is right and proper that our child should be born here, under the rays of the sun."

Toyotama replied equally seriously to Hiko, saying:

"I will agree with your wish if you agree with mine: when the child is being born, I must have complete privacy."

Hiko gave his word and solemnly promised Toyotama that she would be absolutely alone for the birth of their child. In addition to this promise he said he would build her a pretty little pavilion for her personal use, and he vowed never to enter it.

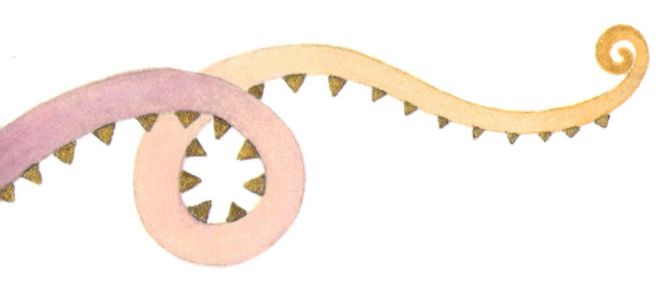

Hiko did indeed build a private garden house for his wife. He asked the kindly clever cormorant who had been so helpful in finding his brother's silver fish hook if she would gift some of her feathers to help him. Thus the pretty little pavilion, its roof decorated with cormorant feathers, was finished on the day of the child's birth.

Toyotama went inside and closed the door.

In honour of his vow, her husband waited outside.

Unknown to him, Toyotama had realised that to safely deliver their child she would have to revert to her natural state of a *tatsu* – a serpent-dragon of the sea. She wanted privacy because she was unsure of her husband's reaction if he saw her in dragon form.

Hours passed, with Hiko becoming more and more curious, and more and more impatient.

Finally, the child was born and Toyotama exclaimed loudly in joy.

Hearing his wife's cry, Hiko rushed to the pretty little pavilion and flung open the door.

A long serpent-dragon was coiled upon the floor cuddling his baby son. Hiko saw that it was his wife and was struck silent with terror.

The dragon lifted her head and anguish filled her heart. Seeing Hiko's stricken look, Toyotama understood that she could not live with a man who viewed her with such fear and had dishonoured her by breaking his solemn vow.

Thus she said goodbye to her husband and, shedding many tears, agreed that it was best for their baby son to be brought up on dry land.

Toyotama returned to her father's magnificent underwater palace. She decided that never again would she take on human form or visit the land. But she arranged that her little cousin Tamayori would assume human form and go to Hiko's home to be her baby son's companion. Over the years as the two children grew up together, they fell in love and in time they married. To them was born a boy child, whom they named Jimmu.

Eventually Jimmu became the first emperor of Japan – with, according to legend, dragon blood flowing in his veins.

The Imperial House of Japan has lasted for well over 2,000 years, making it the oldest continuous hereditary monarchy in the world where royal rule is passed from one family member to another.

Nowadays, on February 11th, Japan has an annual holiday to mark National Foundation Day as a celebration of their nation and of the accession of the legendary first emperor, Jimmu — grandson of Toyotama-hime, Dragon Princess of the Sea.

Lord Krishna and Kaliya Naag

The Bhagavata Purana, a celebrated text of Hindu sacred literature, contains stories featuring Lord Krishna – a deity both powerful and playful.

In Indian folklore a 'Naag' is a huge water-snake dragon with a hooded head like a cobra.

This story is a retelling of the tale where Lord Krishna meets the venomous many-headed dragon, Kaliya Naag.

Kaliya Naag: **Kahl**-ee-a **Na**hg

The banks of the Yamuna River was a favourite place for young cattle-herders to meet.

During hot weather, while their parents worked in the far fields, they brought their animals to drink from the clear sweet water. In one peaceful spot, where the land swept in a gentle curve, a large pool had formed. Beside this inlet grew an immense

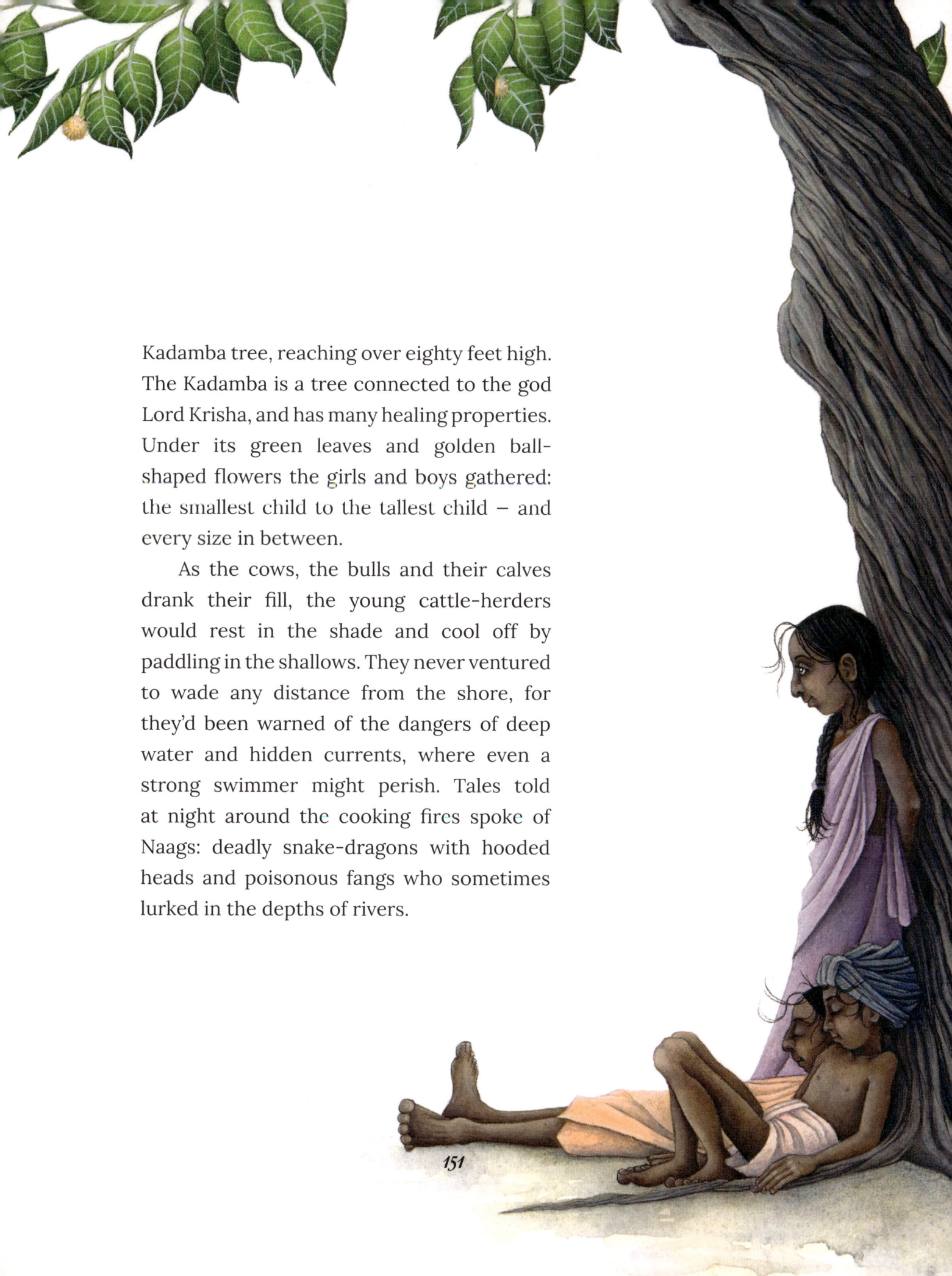

Kadamba tree, reaching over eighty feet high. The Kadamba is a tree connected to the god Lord Krisha, and has many healing properties. Under its green leaves and golden ball-shaped flowers the girls and boys gathered: the smallest child to the tallest child – and every size in between.

As the cows, the bulls and their calves drank their fill, the young cattle-herders would rest in the shade and cool off by paddling in the shallows. They never ventured to wade any distance from the shore, for they'd been warned of the dangers of deep water and hidden currents, where even a strong swimmer might perish. Tales told at night around the cooking fires spoke of Naags: deadly snake-dragons with hooded heads and poisonous fangs who sometimes lurked in the depths of rivers.

Today, the weather was warm, the animals were content, the children had eaten their midday meal and everyone was drowsy with the heat. Thus no one noticed ripples beginning in the middle of the wide river and spreading over the calm surface of the pool. It was only when the littlest calf belonging to the smallest child nervously shuffled close and stamped its feet that the child blinked awake and shouted the alarm.

"A Naag! A Naag!"

The alarm cry awoke the other herders, who scrambled to their feet. A Naag was moving in the river! Long and thick-bodied, it was coming slowly towards them. They could not fully see the approaching monster, but the children knew that they must save their cattle. Grabbing their sticks and switches, they rushed to the edge of the riverbank to shoo the animals away from the water.

Sensing danger, the herd moved. Grunting and snorting, nostrils flaring, dust rose from thundering hooves as they charged off in different directions.

With one voice the children wailed; it would take them days to find their scattered beasts.

"Eeeeeee!" they bawled louder. For, having reached the deepest part of the pool, the Naag broke through the surface – and its full horror was revealed. When the children saw that it had not one but many hooded heads, they screamed in terror. The tallest child yelled:

"It is Kaliya Naag!"

Famed in legend as the most vile and dangerous serpent-dragon, Kaliya Naag had a dozen hooded heads with great jaws and sharp fangs. It rose up, glaring with yellow eyes.

Despite shaking with fear, the children bravely tried to frighten Kaliya Naag by throwing stones: the smallest child threw a pebble, the tallest child hurled a rock.

Kaliya Naag scorned their efforts. Churning the waters into a whirlpool, the serpent-dragon opened its jaws and sprayed jets of venom from its fangs. The stinking poison filled the river. Kaliya Naag wound its tail around its own body and settled down in the centre of the pool.

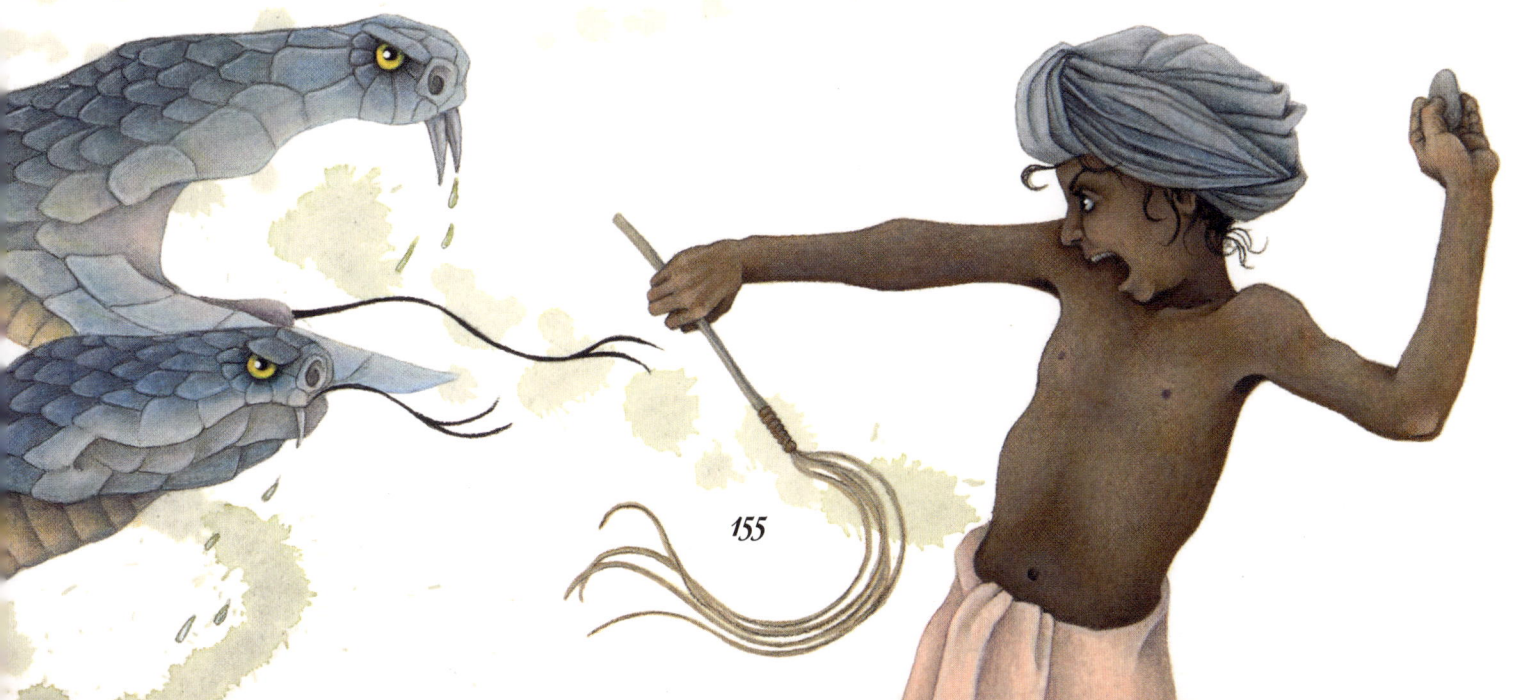

The cattle-herders realised that Kaliya Naag intended to stay and that the river, which provided the good clean water they needed, was lost to them.

In despair they ran back to cluster at the Kadamba tree, in the hope that the sacred tree would protect them.

A soft breeze caused the leaves of the Kadamba tree to rustle.

The smallest child heard the rustling, and then spoke:

"When he was young, didn't the blessed god Lord Krishna play upon his flute while near a Kadamba tree?"

A soft breeze caused the golden ball flowers of the Kadamba tree to nod their heads, and their perfume wafted through the air.

The tallest child smelled the perfume, and then spoke:

"When he was young, didn't the blessed god Lord Krishna use the golden flowers of a Kadamba tree to scent his clothes with the smell of sandalwood?"

All the children, from the smallest child to the tallest child – and every size in between – remembered more stories of Lord Krishna. Of how, when he was young like them, he sat below the Kadamba tree, eating and playing and resting as they did. They recalled the goodness and kindness of Lord Krishna. And they decided that they too would sit below the Kadamba tree.

And so the young cattle-herders, the smallest child to the tallest child – and every size in between – sat in a circle around the Kadamba tree. The children appealed to Lord Krishna to help them, for without fresh water, they and their cattle would surely die.

A soft breeze caused the branches of the Kadamba tree to tremble.

Suddenly, from above the children's heads, came the sound of laughter. Glancing up they saw, perched among the branches, a young lad with mischief on his face and a merry smile on his lips. He wore robes of russet-red and in his hand was a flute.

"Lord Krishna!" they cried. "Krishna! Krishna!" From the smallest child to the tallest child – and every size in between – they squealed in delight and waved their hands in excitement.

Krishna played music until they quietened. Then, tucking his flute inside his tunic and securing his robes, Krishna climbed to the topmost branch of the Kadamba tree and jumped into the pool to confront Kaliya Naag.

Kaliya Naag had been watching with staring eyes and, as Krishna entered the water, the hoods of every one of its heads drew back, preparing to attack. Deftly Krishna slipped from side to side, avoiding each attempt. Thrashing the waves, Kaliya Naag rapidly struck again and again, but Krishna was too swift. Kaliya Naag swivelled its whole body to the surface and tried to wrap itself around Krishna. Lord Krishna held his breath, flipped in the water and ducked under the serpent-dragon. In a daring, darting movement, Krishna grasped the end of Kaliya Naag's tail.

The children cheered as Krishna ascended into the air to hover over the many heads of Kaliya Naag. With one hand Krishna kept a firm grip of the serpent-dragon's tail; with the other he took out his flute and began to play a tune.

Kaliya Naag stretched and writhed to get free, but Krishna did not let go. Poison poured from the fangs of Kaliya Naag. The waves boiled green and brown and blood-orange, foaming with filthy scum.

Expertly, Krishna trod upon a single head of Kaliya Naag. He played more quickly on his flute and, like lightning, skipped to the next head, to beat it down too with his feet.

Thus, keeping time to his music, faster and faster Krishna danced upon the many heads of Kaliya Naag. He was fleet of foot, and with nimble steps he escaped Kaliya Naag's snapping jaws and sharp fangs.

On and on Krishna played his flute and danced. Hour after hour he played and danced, until, one by one, each head of Kaliya Naag drooped in surrender.

The sun was setting, the sky glowing deepest pink, when the last of Kaliya Naag's heads was bent in submission. The jaws stopped snapping and no more venom spouted from its fangs.

As Kaliya Naag sank in the water, so Krishna grew in stature. Finally, Krishna ceased playing and dancing and, in a mighty voice, threatened to destroy Kaliya Naag.

However, the defeated Kaliya Naag replied to Lord Krishna in this way:

"Oh, Master of Time and Seasons and Knower of All, I was created as a serpent-dragon, and consequently I have the nature of a serpent-dragon. I am as I am. And so I ask you, Lord Krishna, do I have your Mercy or your Punishment?"

Lord Krishna pondered on the words of Kaliya Naag before he made his judgement:

"I have listened to your plea, Kaliya Naag. Therefore, I direct you to go now to a far island in the Great Ocean, and henceforth dwell there as a serpent-dragon. You must leave the pure river water for the people, plants and animals to enjoy."

The cattle, hearing the voice of Lord Krishna, were returning, and their lowing echoed in the evening air. Weeping in thanks and happiness, the children ran to meet the cows and the bulls with their calves.

The Yamuna River flowed on, cleansing the poison from the pool, and became pure again, and the young cattle-herders brought their animals to drink from the clear sweet water. There they gather to eat and play and rest below the Kadamba tree: from the smallest child to the tallest child – and every size in between!

There are various versions of the story of Kaliya Naag and Lord Krishna. Their encounter is often seen as the battle between darkness and light – Kaliya Naag representing cruelty and selfishness, with Krishna embodying goodness and joy. In the end the dragon is banished to allow love to flourish.

Lord Krishna is the god of compassion, protection, tenderness and love, and is often depicted playing the bansuri, a kind of Indian flute. His birthday is celebrated every year on Krishna Janmashtami, a festival involving singing, dance and drama.

Author's note

It has been a privilege to work with two of my great loves: stories and dragons. Stories renew us, connect us and allow us to grow. Retelling stories keeps them alive; it lets them find new eyes and ears. Dragons urge us to new feats of courage, inspire us to stay firey, and enable us to connect with otherworldliness.

The stories in *An Illustrated Treasury of Dragon Tales from Around the World* have roots in a lifetime of travelling, listening and reading. I feel great gratitude for the storytellers who came before me, and respect for the cultures from which these tales emerge. It is an honour to retell them for children everywhere.

Illustrator's note

It has been such a joy to illustrate these dragons from all over the world. Whatever they symbolise, dragons continue to fascinate and intrigue, and they hold great cultural significance and resonance. I am immensely grateful to the storytellers and tradition bearers who have kept the dragons with us. May they continue to flourish...

About the creators of
*An Illustrated Treasury
of Dragon Tales*

Theresa Breslin

Theresa Breslin OBE is a highly acclaimed, Carnegic Medal-winning author, who has published over fifty books for children and young adults. She lives in Scotland and travels extensively to share stories. Her work has been filmed for television, adapted for stage and radio, and translated into many languages. Theresa worked as a librarian before becoming a full-time writer. She is passionate about children's literature and literacy.

Kate Leiper

Kate Leiper is a Kate Greenaway Medal-longlisted illustrator and artist based in Edinburgh, Scotland. She studied at Gray's School of Art in Aberdeen, and her work has been exhibited in galleries from London to the north of Scotland. She has been commissioned for projects by the Scottish Storytelling Centre and the Royal Lyceum Theatre. Inspirations for her work range from Scottish folklore, to tales from the Far East, to Shakespeare.

Praise for the Illustrated Treasuries of Scotland collection

'The castles of Scotland are storied places – literally – as we learn from Theresa Breslin's engaging narrative, with dramatic pictures by Kate Leiper.'
The Wall Street Journal

'A sublime collection of folk stories... Theresa Breslin's pristine, sparkling retellings are accompanied by enchanting illustrations from Kate Leiper.'
The Guardian

'Lively yarn-spinning, delightful illustrations and handsome bookmaking make a winning combination.'
Kirkus Reviews

'Theresa Breslin brings an array of creatures to life with her assured and captivating storytelling, and she places a child at the heart of each tale.'
Julia Donaldson

'This is a lovely book enhanced with the most beautiful illustrations. Folk stories have not lost their appeal in the modern world – it is books like this that will keep them alive.'
Alexander McCall Smith

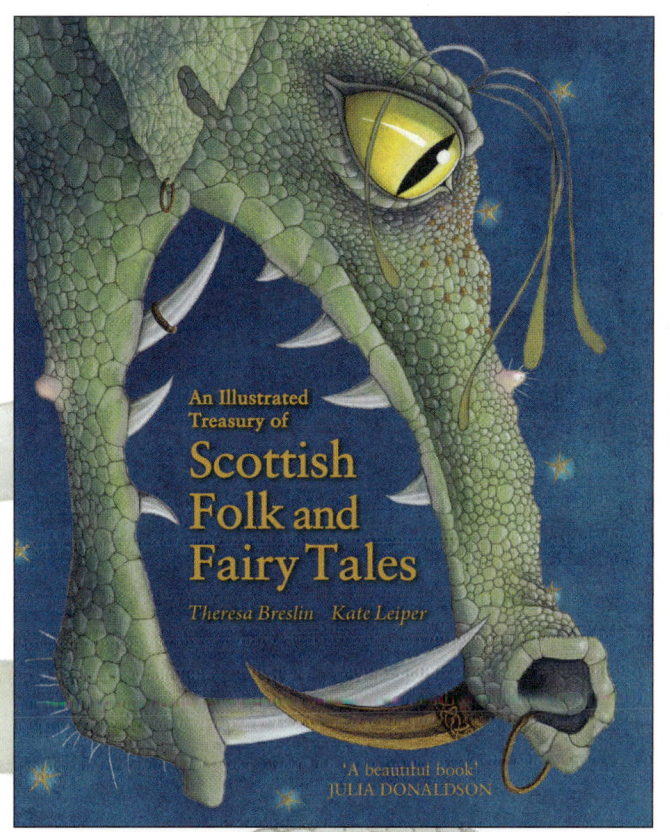
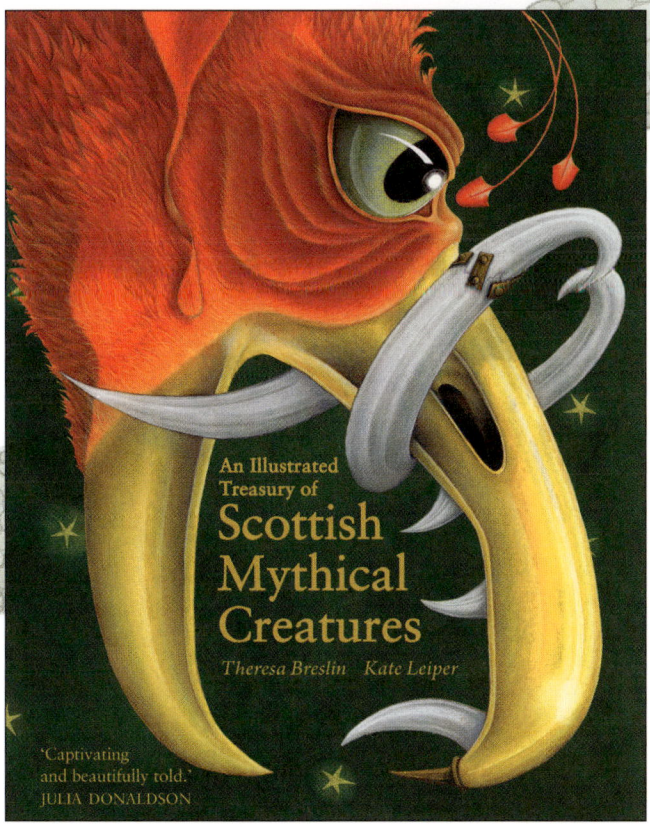
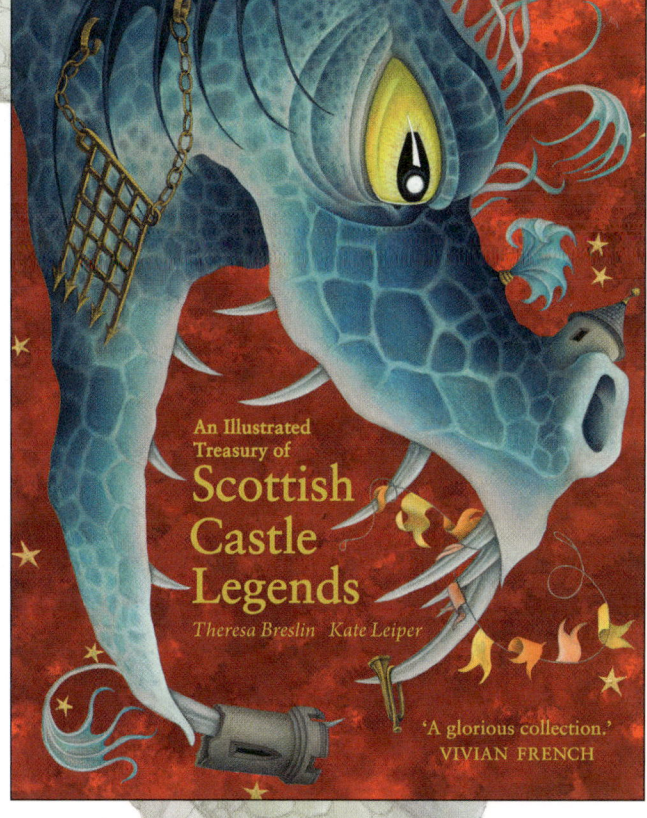

florisbooks.co.uk